THEY WILL DROWN IN THEIR MOTHERS' TEARS

THEY WILL DROWN IN THEIR MOTHERS' TEARS

JOHANNES ANYURU

Translated from Swedish by
SASKIA VOGEL

TWO LINES
PRESS

First published as: *De kommer att drunkna i sina mördrars tårar*

Published by Norstedts, Sweden, in 2017
Published in agreement with Norstedts Agency

Two Lines Press
582 Market Street, Suite 700, San Francisco, CA 94104
www.twolinespress.com

ISBN: 978-1-949641-08-0
Ebook ISBN: 978-1-931883-90-0

Library of Congress Cataloging-in-Publication Data

Names: Anyuru, Johannes, 1979- author. | Vogel, Saskia, translator.
Title: They will drown in their mothers' tears / by Johannes Anyuru;
translated by Saskia Vogel.
Other titles: De kommer att drunkna i sina mördrars tårar. English
Description: San Francisco, CA: Two Lines Press, 2019. | "Originally
published as De kommer att drunkna i sina mördrars tårar"--Title page verso.
Identifiers: LCCN 2019016023 | ISBN 9781931883894 (hardcover)
Subjects: | GSAFD: Dystopias.
Classification: LCC PT9877.1.N98 D413 2019 | DDC 839.73/8--dc23
LC record available at https://lccn.loc.gov/2019016023

Cover design by Gabriele Wilson
Cover photo by World History Archive / SuperStock
Typeset by Sloane | Samuel

Printed in the United States of America

3 5 7 9 10 8 6 4 2

The cost of this translation was defrayed by a subsidy from the Swedish Arts Council, gratefully acknowledged. This project is also supported in part by an award from the National Endowment for the Arts.

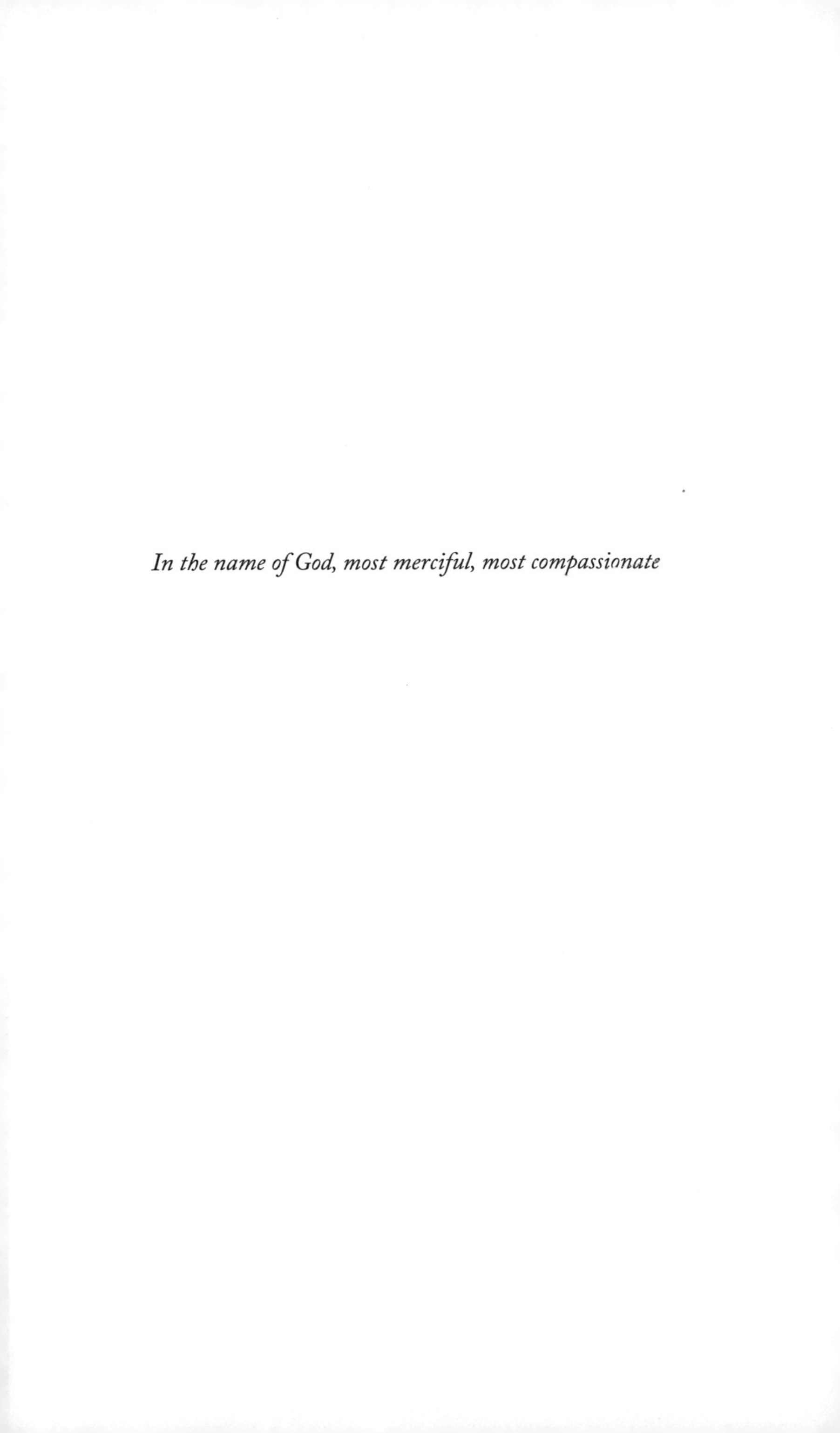

In the name of God, most merciful, most compassionate

There is no such thing as Guantanamo in the past
or Guantanamo in the future.
There is no time,
because there is still no limit to
what they can do.

PRISONER
freed after thirteen years
in Guantanamo Bay

What occurred inside the houses?
Practically nothing.
It went too rapidly to really happen.
Imagine an alarm clock on a nightstand
set to measure out the time in seconds
is caught off guard by its own liquefaction
and then boils up and whirls away as gas
and all this in a millionth of a second.

HARRY MARTINSON
Aniara, sixty-seventh song

Wind comes blowing in. It lifts up sand from the playground in front of the apartment blocks and a scattering of dried grass. The two girls on the old swings swing higher.

I watch them through the window. Their laughter doesn't reach me, but I hear hoarse panicked screams, rattling machine gun fire, objects clattering, bodies flying.

This is her first memory: veils of snow whipping the hospital wings, the parking lot and poplars, the roadblocks. Before that: nothing, actually.

She shuts her eyes. Amin keeps repeating the name he's given her. Nour. Only when hysteria creeps into his voice does she open her eyes again.

"Did you remember something new?" Face drawn, mouth tense, he's sitting next to her in Hamad's white Opel. The backseat is shedding foam-rubber crumbs that stick to their clothing.

She shakes her head.

In the driver's seat, Hamad starts talking, hurrying them, and Amin wets his lips; hands trembling, he switches on the cellphone duct taped to the metal pipes on her vest. She is sitting perfectly still. Outside, stray snowflakes float past a yellow brick wall. If she were to type the four-digit code into the phone's keypad, the metal pipes would explode, flinging out as many nails and bullets as fit in two cupped hands, and the shockwave would break bones and pulp the organs of anyone within a five, maybe ten, meter radius. Texting the code to the cellphone would have the same result.

They get out of the car. Hamad has parked on a back-street, hidden by a dumpster. He heaves the large black gym bag out of the trunk. The cold burns her cheeks and hands, she stomps her feet to warm up.

They walk onto Kungsgatan together, but split up in the Saturday crowd. After a few steps she turns around, so Amin stops, hands in his pockets, and pretends to browse the suits in a window display.

She senses that they are interwoven.

She wishes they could have another life.

It's February seventeenth, a little over an hour before the terrorist attack at Hondo's comic book store.

At one point she almost steps in front of a moving street-car—but a woman grabs her coat—the streetcar's screech is shrill and hollow, and she ends up ankle-deep in slush, taking in the gentle snowfall in the darkening afternoon.

Again she tries to remember who she is, where she comes from, but she only gets as far as that room in the hospital, how she got up and stood by the window, leaning on her IV-stand. She remembers the swell and whine of her pulse in her temples and the cool floor beneath her feet.

She'd read that the snow on the hospital that summer night was caused by environmental devastation, or the military manipulating the weather, or it wasn't even snow at all, but some sort of leakage from a chemical plant.

The woman who grabbed her before she stepped into the street touches her arm again and says something she doesn't catch; the voice is dulled and distant and when she offers no response the woman walks off. Yet another streetcar passes, people go around her on the crosswalk.

At least she's pretty sure she comes from here. Gothenburg. And that her mother is dead. Has died somehow. Was run over. No. Can't remember. She balls her fists, opens them.

A single event can awaken the world.

She's on the move again, back in the stream of shoppers, teenagers in puffy winter jackets, couples with strollers.

Outside the comic book store's propped-open door, a garden candle flickers uneasily in the twilight. Behind it, a handwritten sign:

Tonight at 17:00 Göran Loberg will be signing his latest comic book and discussing the limits of free speech with Christian Hondo.

When she crosses into the light, she starts sweating, because it's crowded and because there's a bomb vest hidden under her winter coat.

Because of what's coming.

She riffles through a box of comic books so as not to draw attention to herself, picks one out, flips through it.

One single act, if it's radical enough, pure enough, can communicate with the world's stateless masses, reestablish ties between the caliphate and the Muslims who've been led astray, increase the influx of new recruits, and turn the tide of the war.

Hamad's words. Hamad's thoughts.

She keeps flipping.

In the comic book, needle-shaped vehicles pass plantations and clouds of burning gas. Men in bulky, intricate spacesuits cross surreal desert landscapes. She's surprised how childish the pictures are.

It actually makes her laugh, and that gives her pause.

She wonders if her body heat can detonate the pipe bombs.

One: she knows she is Muslim. Two: Swedes have killed Muslims in some sort of camp. Three: there's this name, not hers, but it means something—Liat, someone she loved. Four: Swedes are pretending it's peacetime, and that the death camps don't exist. Five: she has talked it all through with Amin, trying to figure it out.

Hamad arrives. Snow blows in through the door that's slamming shut. He and Amin shaved off their beards the night before, and his bare cheeks makes her think of a bird skull—he looks bony and cruel. He's wearing a black quilted jacket and a blue beanie with the logo of an American hockey team on it—a shark—which he takes off and stuffs in his pocket. By the cash register, he puts a black gym bag down at his feet.

Thirty or so people are in the store, standing around in groups or sitting on folding chairs, their outerwear balled in their arms. Christian Hondo, the shop owner, a long-haired man in a worn yellow T-shirt, turns on the microphone. Feedback wails from the two speakers that have been set out for the event.

"I suppose it's time to say hello and welcome to you all." The voice sounds flat and booming, doubled, as it spills from the speakers.

Göran Loberg emerges from a door behind the cash register. The audience turns around expectantly, their attention verging on devotional.

Loberg is older than Hondo, around sixty, stooped and weatherbeaten. She notices something hard about his mouth, contempt or ire. Bushy white hair, plaid shirt. He puts a notebook and pen on the table.

"We're here to discuss your latest project," says Hondo, "*The Prophet*, your collected satirical comic strips, which were published weekly online, and which contain caricatures of the Prophet Mohammed and other, shall we say…objects of blasphemy?"

Loberg nods and scratches his stubble; his entire being emanates sloppiness and a flighty disinterest in himself and his surroundings. She's at the back of the venue. She misses some of what they're saying. It sounds like they're in another room, like their voices don't match their bodies. Floating sounds.

Hondo unrolls a poster. Holds it up for the audience to see.

A group of turban wearing, hook-nosed men are bent in prayer with cruise missiles stuck in their anuses.

It's like she's out of her body, watching herself like in a dream.

The bomb vest is strapped tight across her chest.

One: she can't remember her name. Two: she doesn't remember her real parents, whom she believes were murdered. Three: when she looks in the mirror she sees the wrong face. Four: she sometimes gets a feeling, like right now as she's looking at this scene, that she's been here before, here where an important event, a historic event, is being restaged.

She notices that Amin has come in and positioned himself by the front door. His face is slick with sweat even though he's just come in from the cold. Several people in the store seem worried about the young man, miserable and marked for death, and whisper to each other. Amin glances in her direction but pretends not to recognize her.

She goes over to him.

"Amin," she hisses. He ignores her, unsure of how to react: the plan was to spread out in the venue and wait for it to fill up. They are absolutely not supposed to be talking to each other.

"Amin. Amin." He doesn't even look at her. Reluctantly he lets her grab his hand. She weaves her fingers with his, squeezes. "Everything is wrong." She's not sure what she means by that. "Amin, everything is wrong."

Hamad married her and Amin in his apartment a few months ago and she has been carried to this point by terrible premonitions, by her sense that she and Amin and maybe also Hamad belong together, and that she is on a mission.

"We should bail," she hisses, and next to Amin a man in a black sweater, coat draped over his arm, gives them an irritated look. She doesn't let it faze her. "Let's bail," she says, and only then does Amin allow himself to react—he tears his hand free, grabs her arm, and glares at her. Then he gives her a gentle shove, half to get rid of her and half to get her to remember the plan.

They're supposed to spread out and wait.

Over at the table, Hondo is saying it's not that he hates religion, but he does operate from what he calls a traditionally subversive perspective, a sentiment she doesn't understand and can't contextualize, "a libertine perspective," the voice says, buzzing with treble, "a sort of trash gallery."

She shuts her eyes. The rays of a tender headache rise to the surface then fade. One thing she hasn't told Amin is that ever since Hamad laid out the plan, she's been picturing the headlines. It's like she can already remember what's going to be written about this, afterward.

Like: *Terrorist Couple Tied the Knot before the Attack. See Their Wedding Pictures Inside.*

When she opens her eyes Hondo has unrolled another poster—an old woman on a bridge points a machine gun at a crowd. On the banner behind her: *Refugees Welcome*.

"You received a number of threats as a result of these illustrations."

"Anyone who hasn't suffered from death threats hasn't

said anything essential," Loberg says, straightening his glasses. The people around her laugh. She thinks they look waxen and ghostly, like their skin is giving off a gray deathly sheen. The laughter dies out. People scratch themselves, write in notepads, lean forward, cross their arms.

She thinks: they'll all be dead in under an hour.

It happens without warning, about twenty minutes into the discussion. Loberg is talking about how art must expand, expansion is the constituent characteristic of art, when his train of thought is interrupted by an indistinct cry that comes from a man in the crowd, *he* or *wha*. . .or maybe he's screaming *gun* in English?

She hears the cry and thinks he's shouting in English because he assumes Amin, who has pulled a gun from his pants in one flitting gesture, is not Swedish.

Gun. She hears the word and she hears the shot, and a woman in the front row adopts the brace position, like before a plane crash.

She is close enough to smell the gunpowder, and it's that smell rather than the loud bang that makes her realize the attack has in fact begun.

Amin stays still, gun raised. The shot has left a smoking hole in one of the ceiling tiles above his head. She tries to catch his eye, but his gaze is fixed on some point in front of or far behind her.

People are already leaving their seats. They're heading for the exit, feet tangling in the folding chairs, but they turn back when they see Amin. Many are pitiful and clumsy, they don't know where to go, spinning around, knocking magazines and paperbacks off the shelves. Objects seem heavier now. Time drags then flies, the actions unfold like connected sheets. A guy with a canvas bag and a Mohawk tries to leave through the door behind the cash register but Hamad pushes him down—the sound of his head slamming against the corner of the checkout counter is awful, then he lands on the floor.

Worship God so much they think you're crazy.

Sitting at the table, Hondo is serene. As though he thinks this is planned, part of the event—he's even grinning self-consciously as he takes it all in. Their eyes meet.

Around them, people are stumbling and crawling over each other as though the floor itself were careening.

Hamad is shouting and his shouting finally registers with her; she realizes he's been shouting for a while. She can't make out the words; she can only take in the fact that he's shouting. An irregular drawn-out sound.

A woman, face bloody, is on the floor. She grabs another woman's sweater to try and pull herself up. Someone is hiding in a corner, behind a drift of comic books, she can see a shoe sticking out, a black winter boot—a crying man trips over it.

Hamad jumps on the checkout counter and takes a machine gun from his black gym bag; he holds it over his head like he's showing off a spoil of war or a newborn baby, and now she can hear what he's shouting, not words, but *yo, yo, yo*.

He delivers a few swift kicks to the cash register, which crashes to the floor, scattering coins and bills.

"You desecrate Islam!" Finally spitting out the words, his voice cracks in a raspy howl—the word *Islam* escapes as a pained moan. Fumbling, he takes another machine gun from the bag. She tears off her coat, throws it on the floor, and walks toward him. Again she feels like she's watching herself from outside her body. And that her feet aren't really on the ground. She receives the weapon, clicks off the safety.

Hamad hands her a second machine gun, which she's

supposed to give to Amin. Her coat discarded, the sight of the bomb vest makes people cry out. They fall over themselves and each other, clearing a path for her as she walks toward Amin, who's standing guard at the front door.

It's Hamad who cut the pipes, filled them with nails and projectiles, and made the explosive out of household chemicals. He hung the bombs on three regular fishing vests.

She wonders if the dizziness, everything spinning around and around faster, has something to do with God.

If God is with them.

A few weeks ago, they went to the forest. They drove for over an hour into the countryside on pitted forest roads to practice shooting machine guns. It was only when she felt the weapon buck, smelled the gunpowder, and saw the spiteful flicker leave the barrel that she understood what she was about to do. That it was real. She stood there, ears ringing, the trees glowing in the headlights, pale and ghostly.

This is really happening. We're doing it.

Amin sticks the pistol in his pants and hangs the machine gun from his shoulder. She gives him a sisterly hug. She wants to connect with the feeling that they are really doing this, doing what they had planned, but she still doesn't really feel present. It's more like she's inside a memory.

One: she's doing this out of revenge, because the Swedes killed her mother. She believes this to be true. Two: wrong, this is a mission. She's doing this because she saw Amin on the train one rainy afternoon and knew he would lead her to her destiny, and everything that has happened since has brought her here, to Hondo's, where she's going to do something important, something she can't remember.

Three: the name. Liat. She has to find Liat. Save Liat.

She rubs her temples.

There's unrest at the checkout. Hamad jumps down and runs through the door leading to the storeroom and staff toilet. Shots ring out, loud bangs, three in quick succession. Some people in the store scream and she tries to hush them, awkwardly and embarrassed at first, then with increasing aggression:

"Quiet. Keep quiet. Yo. Yo!"

It's no help. Weeping all around her. Why does she keep feeling like she's remembering this as it's happening?

Hamad walks backward through the door. He's dragging Loberg by the collar, one of the man's legs is leaving a bloody trail on the floor. Like someone painting with a broad brush.

One: she only has Amin and Hamad, and this violence, this revenge she is taking because of unclear assaults in her past.

She becomes aware of a crowd. They've gathered outside the store's window, beyond the shelves of comic books and collectible toys, a cluster of shadows; and right then, as she's looking out, the first police car arrives, blue lights blaze and spin through the winter night, making the reflection in the window disappear, reappear, disappear.

She should've left.

Hamad pushes Loberg up against the checkout counter and presses the barrel of the gun to his forehead. She watches it happening and feels paralyzed. Why was it snowing the night she came to? Why doesn't she remember her real name?

Hamad butts Loberg in the temple with the weapon and he drops. Hamad doesn't shoot.

Get it on film.

Loberg is slumped against the counter, body limp, legs sticking out, glasses broken. He's staring at her. Nearby, Hamad is forcing the hostages to their knees, cuffing them with white plastic zip ties, covering their mouths with silver duct tape and their heads with black canvas bags. He works quickly and when one of them disobeys he gives them a stressed slap.

Loberg has a strip of tape over his mouth but no canvas bag over his head; he's staring at her through the jagged hole smashed in his glasses. She turns away.

She dries her sweaty palms on her pants and takes the cellphone from her pocket.

At the hospital they insisted she was someone else. Called her by a name that was not hers and spoke a language she didn't understand.

She is one of thousands who have been kidnapped and tortured since 9/11. That much she knows.

That much she thinks she knows.

Hamad switches places with Amin at the front door. He'll handle the police while she and Amin make the video.

Amin, stance wide, poses in front of the black flag. The balaclava he's wearing was bought at an Army surplus store along with the fishing vests. However, the black canvas bags they've put over the hostages' heads are stolen: pillowcases from a furniture store.

"In God's name," says Amin, who, like she and Hamad, has taken his jacket off, exposing another bomb vest. "We send greetings to our brothers on the front lines."

She zooms out. Even so, she has to take a few steps back so the camera can take in the whole scene.

She's the one who made the flag, based on pictures she found on the web. Four cut-up trash bags pieced together with black tape, the white emblem painted by hand. It's hanging behind Amin on a bookcase.

She's responsible for the video. She's live streaming it via a number of social networks and YouTube channels—Hamad has helped her access the right accounts and set up her phone.

Amin takes a piece of paper out of his pants pocket. He reads a sentence in shaky Arabic. Under their black hoods a few hostages start crying again, because of the incredible and frightening power of people with automatic weapons speaking a foreign language, which is easy to mistake for the power of God's word. She sees a man who might be Latin American or Turkish, a student—she noticed he wasn't Swedish before Amin put the hood on him—bend forward as if he were anticipating a sweeping blow from up high.

They spend eight hours a day watching television. And they call us extreme.

They laugh at our religion.

They murder us in Syria, in Iraq, in Afghanistan, in Chechnya, in Palestine.

She tries to get everything on video; it's shaky and blurred.

Amin wanted to steal her a "dope" digital camera, but Hamad said that everything should be filmed with a cellphone.

The format should attest to their modest means.

"In the name of the Leader of the Faithful. In the name of every Muslim's honor..." He cuts off his speech and goes over to Loberg, who's still sitting against the checkout counter. Through the camera's eye, there's something disoriented and dazzled about him. Because he will die first, and because his death is meaningful precisely because of who he is—unlike the other hostages, who will die because they're nobodies, ordinary infidels, chosen by chance, that is to say, by God—he's not wearing a hood.

Pulling at his rough cotton shirt and spurring him along

by kicking him, Amin leads Loberg over to a spot in front of the flag, a spot she thinks of as a stage. He crawls, hops on his knees, and falls on his face a few times when Amin prods him with the tip of his shoe—it makes Hamad laugh with malicious delight from his post at the front door.

They are simple people who exist beyond the lies and distortions of the media machine.

Soon they will be in paradise.

Still no communication with the police outside.

Amin returns to his spot by the black flag. He straightens his balaclava, pinches it at the cheeks—apparently it's itchy.

The martyr leaves this world before the first drop of his blood hits the floor.

She watches Amin on the screen, with Loberg kneeling in front of him, and to banish an awful worry that nothing is as it should be, she thinks of paradise and its immense trees—their crowns moving in the wind.

The film is supposed to be pixilated, shaky, with unexpected close-ups of the speaker's shoes and so on—she's following Amin's movements, but the lens captures the comic books spread across the floor, overturned chairs, somebody's elbow, blood splatter from Loberg's leg.

"We have passed judgement on this man, who is known to all of you," Amin says. His body language belies his nerves. He wants to rush it. He's having a hard time sounding slick. "This so-called artist. I mean, this man whom we have judged. For blasphemy and dishonor. He has not honored our Prophet."

She zooms in on Amin's eyes, staring through the narrow opening in the balaclava. She feels dizzy, looks up from the bright display, and blinks away the flickering spots. The headlines and news reports in her head, *yani*, a voice saying we would like to offer a warning to our more sensitive viewers. You know: sick.

Who is she?

She glances at Hamad, who is peering out the window.

Hard to see what's going on outside with the emergency vehicles' blue lights sweeping through the store.

Breaking: Terrorist Attack in Gothenburg.

The light through the cellphone screen has a greenish tint and she focuses on the action there. She wants to feel how it disturbs her, which has something to do with her thinking that she's remembering what's happening right before it happens—a phrase Amin uses, a hand gesture—it's like a double exposure, an echo.

"The punishment is death," Amin says on the stage, and Göran Loberg snorts, as though low pressure is drawing the air out of him, and he doubles over from the undeniable power of a worldview that takes it upon itself to rule over life and death.

She recognizes this.

Why does she recognize these scenes?

Amin looks at the figure at his feet with surprise and appreciation. Maybe Loberg needs to vomit, his hair is sticking out in every direction and his bumbling quasi-aristocratic dignity is gone. Mostly he looks like a homeless man who's been slapped around after having been caught pickpocketing.

"The punishment is death," Amin repeats, stroking the machine gun pensively. He nods to himself, appearing to go through the text in his head.

His face isn't covered to hide his identity. It's covered to show that he's part of an anonymous mass, that he could be anyone. He could be the Muslim sitting next to you on the bus, unemployed and friendly—an ordinary well-mannered young man who gives up his seat for the elderly, most of the time, but who has had it up to here with racism and colonialism.

"The punishment is death," he says for the third time, and laughs.

He is nineteen years old and never finished grade school. He laughs again, louder. He's polite and right now he's between jobs because he hasn't been given a fucking chance, that's the way it is, that's what he usually tells her—the Swedes haven't given him one single tiny fucking chance.

He could be anyone, a guy from Hasselbo who's smoked his share of hash, okay, sure, he's sparked up plenty in the glow of his computer, amid the whirl of local and American trap videos or conspiracy theory videos—the Illuminati and whomever else he was talking about when he was stoned... the Rothschilds—while he fantasized about success and revenge and anything that could speak to the feeling of having been taken for a ride. He does usually get up for the elderly, and even for Swedes, especially for Swedes, to show them what Islam stands for in a world that never rewards goodness.

She keeps watching him on the screen, standing there with his head slightly bowed and laughing a kind of middle-school giggle, so much more pleasurable because right here, right now, is not the time or place.

He picks up one of Loberg's books from the desk and flips through it. The pictures silence his laughter—using his entire body, he demonstrates his disgust for what he's seeing. He holds the pages out to the camera.

Another one of Loberg's pictures: a man with a lampshade on his head, electric shocks being administered through his nipples. The camera's autofocus blurs the speech bubble.

The man's wide-open eyes and mouth shine on a newspaper being read by a burqa-wearing woman in an armchair.

"You want to dishonor Islam!" Amin holds out the pages toward Loberg and says, "Huh? Huh? Huh?" while smacking Loberg on the back of his head and across his face.

One of the male hostages is breathing heavily, panicked—as she turns to look the camera follows along—the black canvas bag is being sucked into the man's nose.

The canvas bag blows out, is sucked back in—he looks like he might actually be suffocating.

She notes the madness in being the armed ones in a room.

Amin flips to another picture, says "Do you?" and Loberg utters a few frightened, lowing sounds in reply, possibly because it's finally dawning on him that he is about to die. Amin jerks his collar to get him to sit up.

He resumes giggling to himself. She zooms in and out at the right times. Amin tugs at Loberg's collar even though the man is already sitting—he's taking something extra out on Loberg that has to do with an old teacher or his pops.

She can't get her head around her lack of compassion. Maybe it has something to do with the camera, how it isolates events from each other and from reality.

She's also familiar, in a secret way, with the cruelty hidden in Loberg's well-ordered world, the one in which he'd just been sitting, joking, and jotting down notes. Maybe that's why she doesn't feel the slightest tenderness for this man's abused body. Because of something heartless and raw hiding in the handshakes and bus schedules and pert comments, something she can feel in her skin and hair.

At some point Amin hit Loberg in the nose, it's bleeding profusely. She angles her camera down and to the side, out of weakness and out of sorrow, in spite of it all, a sorrow over what she's seeing and immortalizing, a sorrow that has nonetheless caught up with her.

Amin has trampled around in the blood from Loberg's wounded leg and has left a trail of sticky, red Nike logos on the gray linoleum floor.

A comic book stuck to his sole flutters.

By now it's around 7:30 p.m. Squad cars and police vans have rolled in, along with several ambulances and a fire truck. The prime minister has been informed and a task force is on its way from Stockholm in a military helicopter.

Her hands are stiff and remote because of adrenaline and shock; she keeps nearly dropping the phone.

Amin takes out a knife—a box cutter with an orange plastic handle. He fiddles with it, sliding the blade out, drawing it in, sliding it out. She's focused on the knife's cold fish-scale shine, but senses movement over by the entrance: Hamad is pressing one of the hostages against the glass while screaming at the police outside in the darkness and snow:

"Back off!" He holds the hostage by the neck: "Back off!" He takes a step back and curls himself around his weapon, ready to fire, feet spread wide—he pushes the barrel into the hostage's neck as a threat, as if to say: *I'll shoot him if they don't obey me*. "Back off!"

She's trying to follow the action with the cellphone camera, but it's hard to know what's key—at one point she decides that a furtive glimpse of Amin is the thing, but he's consumed by the action at the front door, so she pans back to Hamad screaming, weapon still raised—it's the viral cellphone video's hyper-present wired aesthetic—my God, I can't believe my eyes; have to get it on film—she's both perpetrator and witness.

Two policemen from the Gothenburg van have approached, guns drawn, going against established procedures for a hostage situation, and Hamad, who had counted on more or less set responses from the police, is losing it—he shouts again:

"Back off!"

It happens first in her head.

She wants to tell Hamad to get down.

Click on the link to watch the video.

"Hamad!" she manages to say. She sees it first like a memory, a film scene on the backs of her eyelids, then on the cellphone's small screen, and then—mostly a confused afterthought—she looks up and understands that this is really happening.

At first the shots from outside are hollow and faint, what follows is glass shattering and finally a sucking smack.

Harrowing images from the terrorist's own camera.

Hamad's head is flung backward—Hamad with his old white Opel and his stories about Syria—his head is flung backward and on the footage you see part of his scalp fly off—blood and gray mush splash across the boxes of comics. He said it wouldn't happen—the bomb vests were their back-up.

She hears shouts from outside, unclear and mixing with the hostages' voices, which are now screaming, unhinged and shrill, behind strips of duct tape.

What am I doing here?

Everything is wrong.

Wasn't God on Hamad's side?

A voice inside the store shouts that it was one of them, the police shot one of them—it's Loberg shouting, the only hostage who doesn't have a black bag over his head and can orient himself somewhat—probably to calm the others.

She makes her way over to Hamad, crouched so low that at times she's crawling on all fours. She's still holding the cellphone—filming the floor, red speckles, comic book panels.

The body is on its back, arms and legs flung out, breathing fitfully through its mouth, face swollen, bluish.

She thinks she sees a moth, large as her palm, crawling over Hamad's face.

"Turn it off," he says. "Turn it off."

The moth's wings are darkly dappled, brown streaked with blue.

The clamor of time.

She isn't who she appears to be.

Doesn't come from here.

"Turn off the light." The bullet hole in Hamad's cheek is so small you could barely fit a finger in, but blood is streaming from it, pulsing out over his pale, sunken cheek.

Wings trembling, the moth creeps across his forehead and into his hair. She stares at it, frozen. A new memory: A man looking out into the night through a shattered window. Her dad. She remembers her dad. Her mom beside him, knife in hand. She sees them clearly.

What happened to her?

Turn off the light so they don't have anything to aim at. That's what Hamad means.

She points the camera at Amin, who's crouched behind a box of shrink-wrapped comics, the machine gun in his cramped embrace. She hisses his name but he doesn't respond.

She senses a mechanism inside time, a power that sucks everything backward into the dark.

This isn't the first moth she's seen.

Don't think about what it means. It's too late to think.

Too late, Nour.

But her name isn't Nour. That's just a name Amin gave her.

She crawls over to the light switch behind the cash register and turns off the ceiling lights. Then the blue light flashing through the window is the only light in the store.

Hamad's free hand starts fumbling in the air, movements that seem blind. She looks for the moth, but it's gone.

The seconds, a roaring river delta.

On film: the side of Hamad's bloodied face, as though shot in passing. She points the camera at him so she can find comfort through it. The shine of the camera's gaze, its final judgement, and his eye, so close to the lens, no longer belongs to the anatomy of the face, it's something else, inhuman and obscene: the bloodshot, egg-white-soft glassine structure; the eyelid's shimmering pink cusp; the canopy of the iris around the pupil's black hole.

The globe of the eye blinks slowly.

The film recorded at Hondo's as Hamad nears death is streamed by millions around the world, via cellphone, laptop, tablet. Several of the larger news outlets overseas—but no Swedish outlets—put it up in real time.

The eye, moist and dying, blinks ever more slowly.

A thought gets rattled loose from the mire of Amin's mind when he sees Hamad's hand raised in a clawing or penitent gesture, with half his brain splattered across the comics, coins, and bills: Hamad must have gotten contact lenses the same summer he started hanging out on the square.

So many years ago.

He wants to crawl over to Hamad, but he's being held in place by a force beyond his will, a pounding, paralyzing heft—the intimate inertia of survival presses him to the floor.

Blood mixed with cranial grit pools behind Hamad's head.

Remembering that summer.

Hamad went to the same school as he did. He came from the subdivision just east of Hasselbo. Two years older, but nerdy, chubby, acned, he tucked in his shirt and wore glasses. The kind of fool Amin and his friends would have messed with during break time. Then the summer between ninth grade and high school Hamad turned up in Hasselbo wearing a black windbreaker and tracksuit pants and started hustling hash, and guess if that motherfucker got on Amin's nerves? It was so obvious he was fronting with those clothes and acting all hard and shit—for so long Hamad had been among those who were not wanted here, directionless, smoking in the light of tobacco shops and in a colder light of a fortified anger that came out during fights with chain-wrapped knuckles. Yeah, this is what Hamad was all about even though he came from a nice neighborhood and had a dad with a good job—like at a bank or something—who was around. And he'd go on and on about the price of an eighth or a kilo—it made Amin want to stomp his ass. But at the same time…at the same time Hamad was older and had managed to gain the respect of other older kids. Amin started hearing that Hamad was helping set up break-ins at his own dad's company and was raking it in for some O.G.s.

That was one summer.

Now he's on the floor, shot down, and Amin is staring at him, and at "Nour," as he calls the girl he met one rainy day last fall, and Amin's thinking about life, about how it goes.

He thinks about his sister, who was also named Nour. Twirling. Her tiny baby fingers touching his. And the cops pulling him down to the ground, down into the puddles. Digging a knee into his back. Later, of course, that was much later. And of course his pops had left.

That's how it goes.

And he and Hamad got tight eventually, of course, after that nerd proved he could be trusted if shit went down. Some nights, after Amin started working for him, when they were sitting in Hamad's house, when his parents weren't home, dividing up the hash and weed and pills in resealable plastic bags, Amin felt a strange closeness to him *because* he'd been a nerd for all those years. Not that Amin had ever been one. Hell no.

But because sometimes he wished he could be a different person, too.

"God has to touch them," says Hamad, who has grabbed ahold of her pantleg and is tugging at the fabric, scrabbling and desperate. It's like the comic book store is slowly being drained of air. Sitting there hunched over, the weight of the bomb vest feels new, and she sends a thought toward its dark, contained energy. The SWAT team's flickering lights make the shadows beat like wings. The thought of large beastly moths rises up again, and again she pushes the thought back down.

"Touch who?" she asks, and Hamad sounds surprised when he responds:

"All of us. God has to touch everyone."

She calls to Amin, who is hyperventilating and has been for minutes. Eventually he reacts: he pulls the balaclava up to his forehead and takes a couple deep breaths as if he'd just surfaced from the sea.

"Amin," she says, and he stares at her, but instead of answering he raises his weapon over his head and fires off a salvo out the window—he's screaming as he squeezes the trigger, but the scream is drowned out by the roaring shots—the muzzle flash lights up his open mouth.

Her ears keep ringing long after Amin's shots have fallen silent—a drawn, monotone wail—and she turns her head and sees a new constellation in the shop window—seven eight nine bullet holes.

Read all about the terrorist's insane plot.

One: the moth was both real and not real. Two: the moths, which she often sees, are related to a flaw in time. Three: she doesn't remember the first time she saw them. Four: maybe it had already started when she was in the hospital, before she fled that night. Maybe even earlier.

Five: can't remember.

She unfastens the buckles on Hamad's bomb vest and struggles to get it off him. He's heavy and unwieldy in the way the dead are. She calls to Amin again, who gets to his feet, snuffling, and fires his machine gun for a second time, straight up into the ceiling—he seems to take power from its roar and fire.

Halogen lights shatter and rain down on him like smoking crushed eggshells.

"Handcuffs. Handcuffs."

Amin takes a zip tie out of Hamad's black bag and uses it to secure one of the hostages by the door—a short man in a brown blazer. As she hangs the bomb vest on him, she notices that he's peed himself—the urine looks metallic in the flaming blue light, like he's leaking quicksilver.

The infidels push a button in Las Vegas and an entire wedding party is murdered on the other side of the planet. And they call us extreme.

These are Hamad's thoughts inside her brain.

She checks her cellphone to make sure the text message that will detonate the vest is ready to send.

Amin has squatted down next to Hamad and is tugging

and scratching at the dead man's clothes and whispering to him; she goes over to them. She doesn't know why she's still filming, and when Amin looks up at her, straight into the camera, his face is so gaunt she thinks she can see the skeleton behind the flesh, like an x-ray—large dark holes and long bare teeth. The world contracts, becomes a band stretched tight across her temples, the blood pounding. Maybe she and Amin are in fact the ones being held hostage, by the people in here, and by the events taking place and the fear they're spreading.

They wanted to have something to call their own.

They tried to find something true.

She pulls off her own bomb vest. Puts it on another hostage, forces her to climb into the window display—pressing the barrel of her weapon into a woman's back—where she cowers, frightened and out of place among the collectible toys and rare first editions.

She gets the feeling she's done this before.

She returns to Amin and Hamad.

"Everything is wrong," she says again, and Amin sniffs snot back into his nose and tries to speak but it comes out as a long plaintive sound. He clenches his teeth and rocks back and forth. "Amin. Everything is wrong."

He looks at her, eyes red with tears.

"Fam is ice cold," he says. "Yani, soldier. Yani, *askari*, get it?"

She nods, touches his hand, knows he's talking about Hamad, about the square, about the slanging days and chaotic nights before Hamad went to Syria.

"Nobody fucked with him," Amin says. "But then he got all serious, you know? With a girl. Or with that fucking social worker who started talking to him, right?"

The two of them have Hamad's blood on their hands; it's already cold and syrupy.

"Listen to me, Amin. I don't think we should be here. This isn't where we were supposed to end up."

They should've cut and run.

What kind of mission did she think she was on here?

"I've seen it a thousand times," Amin says and squeezes his eyes shut. "Or the guys from the mosque start in on you with their fire and eternity talk. You get soft. And every fool you jumped comes back at you."

"I know, Amin."

"So he left," he says. "He bounced, you know what I'm sayin'? To fucking Syria."

The corpse's face doesn't look like Hamad anymore, it's just an obliterated, stiffening object, but Amin keeps trying to fix it up, put the head straight and raking his fingers through the wet hair. "Then he turned up six months later, saying he missed me at the mosque." Amin laughs at that, empty and worried.

"Why was it snowing?" she asks, because everything inside her is torn up now, and everything is coming out, all the questions she's bottled up just so she can function. "The first thing I remember is that I went to the window, and it was summer, but it was snowing." She's sitting on the other side of Hamad's body. "Why don't I remember who I am, Amin? Why can't I remember where I come from?" She isn't talking to him anymore but to herself, and maybe that's why he finally responds:

"They killed your mother."

"When? When did that happen? Why don't I remember?"

"It's like you said it was. You were in the camp!" His voice is panicked—you can hear it on the film even though the camera has dropped lens-down on the floor. "I love you, Nour." He gets up in a sudden rush of nervous energy, and stares out into the night at the police, the blockade, the winter.

"My name isn't Nour," she says, which is a betrayal.

Nour is the name of his dead sister, not me.

Twirling.

She must remember something: Liat. Save Liat. Save Mom and Dad, even though they're already dead.

She stays put. Amin goes over to Loberg and gives him a few frustrated, unfocused whacks with the butt of the machine gun.

"Camera," he says to her, and then: "Lights." He repeats himself: "Lights. Lights."

She gets up, grabs her phone. Turns on the flashlight, walks through the hostages shining light on the scene—the flag's black plastic surface gleams, cheap and brittle.

See the Terrorist Couple's Private Photos.

Loberg lets himself be dragged by his hair without a sound or struggle.

There's movement behind the register and she hears the door to the storeroom opening and people fleeing, but she doesn't bother to run after them.

Soon it will be over.

I Hid to Survive—The Night of the Bomb in a Hostage's Own Words.

She focuses on the screen, on Amin's shark eyes. The world shrinks into the screen. The screen expands and swallows life.

Amin digs around in his pants pocket and retrieves the knife. He unfolds the blade and pulls Loberg's hair; her nose starts bleeding, hot and wet, from both of her nostrils.

Sometimes her nose bleeds when she remembers something new.

Amin puts the sharpened blade to Loberg's throat, she sees it happening on screen, and she remembers.

At last she remembers where she's seen Amin before.

She stops recording.

2

Tundra, a criminal psychiatric clinic, is situated in the outskirts of the Rävlanda district, an hour's bus ride from Gothenburg. It is comprised of three buildings: two brick ones built in the early '50s, and a larger five-story one in concrete—when seen from above the three pavilions form the letter *H*. The latter was added during the psychiatry reform of the 1960s, and its purpose was, and has remained, to serve as a facility for the nation's most dangerous criminally insane.

All in all Tundra has just over ninety beds, split over six divisions, as well as an investigative unit. It is one of two high-security clinics in Sweden.

I walked beneath the steel palisade, under chestnut trees ravaged by rain, and into the enclosed park that surrounds the three buildings. A man was raking up a half-rotten pile of leaves. I later found out that he was the so-called "Bear Man"—the Nazi who'd killed three people with a machete in Karlshamn the year before. As I passed he stared at me, mouth open and steaming.

At the entrance to the larger building I handed over my sharp objects (keys and pens), putting them in a plastic box, then was searched halfheartedly by one of the male employees, a guard, apparently: since the late '90s everyone employed in the high-risk clinics throughout Sweden wears civilian clothing and can only be distinguished from the patients by the alarm units and swipe cards attached to their belts.

The guard accompanied me down the corridor and up the stairwell. My meeting was to take place in a room that was usually used for group therapy. I saw her through the security glass before I even walked inside. She was sitting still in a blocky, molded-plastic chair. The hood of her gray sweater was up and concealed a snug black hijab. She was swollen around the eyes, presumably a side effect of some medication or other.

My steps on the linoleum floor echoed.

The guard followed close behind; I felt like I was approaching the abyss; I wanted to turn around and go home.

Barely two years had gone by since the attack at Hondo's.

The girl's head was bowed.

According to the passport that was recovered in Amin's apartment after the attack, she was a Belgian citizen. Amin had called her "Nour," but the name on the passport was Annika Isagel.

The guard opened the door with his swipe card. The room smelled of cleaning products, and an old camera, an early digital model, was set up on a tripod in one corner. The doctor who'd written and invited me to visit—the girl had read my books and asked to meet me—was not present, which I found a bit remarkable.

She looked up. Daylight filtered through the reinforced security glass, hazy and flat, it fell across her worn, bulky clothing, across her forehead and cheeks, across that mouth set in concentration, and I don't know what I'd expected of her, but it wasn't tears.

A murderer who'd shed blood in the name of my religion. A demon who'd stolen my face. She was crying, soundlessly, while looking at me.

I stopped in the middle of the room. The guard took a seat in one of the empty chairs. The girl used her sleeve to wipe away the tears.

"*As-salaamu-alaikum.*" Peace. That was the word she used to greet me. The only one of the three terrorists to survive that wintry night of February seventeenth—the first word she said to me was *peace*.

I didn't respond to her greeting. She got up, and even though the movement wasn't especially abrupt it made me shrink and take a step backward. The way my fear registered, behind her half-shut, swollen eyes, was unclear. She went over to a pine bookshelf and picked up a stack of papers. I'd spotted them as I came into the room, because the bookshelf was otherwise empty: there were twenty-some printed pages. I'd assumed it was a forgotten file or notes from group therapy. When she handed them to me I didn't take them; instead, I looked to the guard for guidance. He scratched his blond mustache and shrugged.

"Why did you want to meet me?"

"This is the beginning of it." Her voice wasn't the same as it was on the video of the attack. It was calm, like an ordinary teenage girl from one of Gothenburg's suburbs, a little edgy and shy. "Yani, the first chapter."

"The first chapter of what?"

She studied me with sad tenderness, and I remember thinking something that I would have reason to reflect upon much later: *She's looking at me like she's saying goodbye.*

"The first chapter of my story," she said. I took the pages.

In his email, her doctor explained that she was suffering

from severe undifferentiated schizophrenia with psychotic episodes and hallucinations—maybe it was no wonder that after reading my books, she'd started writing one herself. I sat down in one of the empty chairs and flipped through the pages without reading them, and then posed the question I'd come to ask:

"What actually happened that night? After you turned off the camera?"

She went over to the window, watched something outside. In the daylight she looked sleep-deprived and exhausted.

Before coming to Tundra, I'd read almost everything that had been written about the attack: in print, on news websites, and on social networks. The girl in front of me had grown up in Brussels and converted to Islam at fourteen; according to her family it was so she could be with a boyfriend she'd had at the time, a guy her age with Moroccan roots. She left home after a fight and moved in with her boyfriend's family, and soon after that she disappeared. Her parents suspected that the boyfriend had hurt her and reported her disappearance to the police. Only after the boyfriend was in custody for several weeks did it come to light that she'd been arrested by the VSSE, the Belgian State Security Service, and had been secretly transferred to the al-Mima prison in Jordan. There she was interrogated by the VSSE, and presumably the French as well, in cooperation with consultants and specialists from K5GS. K5GS was a military company headquartered in Amsterdam that, in addition to working alongside NATO-soldiers stationed in the Middle East and Africa, provided security solutions for public transportation systems in several European cities and conducted data analysis from a complex in London. Eventually her parents, through persistent legal work, had her returned to Belgium, but she was in terrible shape from her stay at al-Mima and was hospitalized in Brussels. This was about two years before the attack on Hondo's. For several months the doctors described her state as catatonic: she was awake but unresponsive to external stimuli; she didn't speak, didn't eat on her own, and never even got out of either bed or the wheelchair her visitors sometimes pushed her around in. Her pupils reacted to light, but other than that her reflexes were shut down or numb.

On the evening of June eleventh, one and a half years before the attack, she got out of her sickbed and went over to the window. She began sobbing and collapsed to the floor.

In the following weeks she became more and more aware of her surroundings, but still didn't speak with anyone.

She fled the hospital in the middle of August and turned up in Gothenburg three months later: she'd been fined a few times for fare skipping on buses and streetcars.

One final detail, the importance of which remains undetermined, is that her waking up coincided with a meteorological anomaly: the same night she got out of bed and looked out the window, snow rolled in over the Northeast of Brussels, even though it was the middle of summer.

"Can we talk about something else first?" she said in response to my question about the events of February seventeenth. I shrugged; she said: "There was a tree behind the apartment building we lived in."

"In Brussels? Was that when you lived with your family or with your boyfriend?" I had a vague memory of a cement colossus set against a gray sky, a pretty typical piece of scene-setting from the articles about her life.

"I never had a boyfriend," she said. "Just Amin."

"I'm talking about the Moroccan guy. The one who got you to convert to Islam."

"It's like…that's not me." She chewed on her lower lip. "I never lived in Brussels."

"What do you mean that isn't you?" I asked.

She picked underneath her nails, an attempt to fill the room's oppressive, watchful stillness with a small nervous tic.

"I look in the mirror and that's not me," she said after a while. "It's not my face." So much for an explanation. She continued: "It was a willow tree."

"A willow tree?"

"Behind our apartment."

Her gaze drifted through the foggy reinforced glass. She seemed to be holding back an incredible inner pressure.

I felt like I was having a meeting with evil right there in that room, like a single glance would leave a stain on my soul.

In one sense she was a prime example of a young person who'd been drawn into religious zealotry. Before she got together with the Moroccan guy in Belgium she had, according to her family, been fascinated by Tibetan Buddhism and yoga, and on one occasion she'd overdosed on DMT, a drug that in certain circles is said to have mind-expanding properties.

One thing complicating this picture was the fact that she did not speak the language she should—Flemish—and as far as I knew, there was no reasonable explanation as to why she could speak Swedish.

During the first phase of the trial—it had of course been held behind closed doors—she'd made certain assertions, the exact nature of which were not revealed to the public. These had led to the psychiatric evaluation, which in turn had ended with her being placed in Tundra's division for its most dangerous patients.

"My mother loved that willow tree," she said. She was

slurring slightly, and I thought this too might be a side effect of her medication. "I liked resting my head on her stomach and looking up into its leaves." Her eyes, fixed on something outside the window, were dark and anxious. "That tree used to make me think of death," she said. "The light through the leaves, you know?"

"Yes," I said.

Extensive materials had leaked about K5GS soon after the girl was set free. Primarily videos depicting daily operations at the al-Mima prison: people with electrodes fixed to their shaved heads, people submerged in water or being shot through with an electric current. Some of the prisoners in al-Mima, in addition to the waterboarding and abuse, were said to have been subjected to neurological experiments.

I wondered what happened to her out there, in the desert.

"Do you want me to write a book about you? Is that why I'm here?"

She nodded. There was something ambiguous about the gesture, as if she wanted to add something but couldn't get it out. The silence between us thickened.

"I wonder if it made Mom think of the same thing. That willow tree. If it made her think of death, too, and if that's why she liked it. My real mom, I mean." She glanced at me in the chair and waited. "My real dad wrote poetry. Like you." She smiled as she said it.

Much of what happened on February seventeenth after she turned off the camera on her cellphone was unknown to the public. Some sort of internal conflict had erupted.

A private video existed that had been shot through one of the store windows, jerky and blurred by sudden movements and flares of light.

Amin looked like he was about to slit Loberg's throat,

but the girl who was now in front of me had raised her machine gun and shot him.

Of course, countless analyses had been made of that video—attempts to get to the bottom of what had happened. In some versions, the film had been slowed down and the action was played back frame by frame, and others zoomed in on Amin's face or hand or the girl's to be discussed for hours, by experts on terrorism, psychology, radical Islam.

"If you want, I can write more," she said, pointing to the papers I was holding. "If you come back."

I wondered what connection was being made by the simple fact of me being there in the room with her—if I was becoming an accomplice to something. I folded the papers in half, got up, and on my way out the door she said what I assumed she'd been keeping in for the entire conversation:

"I'm not from here."

My back was to her. "So where do you come from, then?"

Her reply startled me:

"The Rabbit Yard."

I took the bus through the barren West Coast landscape, home to Isra and our daughter. I read the girl's papers and tried to understand what I was up against. This was during that long, warm fall when the government was considering declaring a state of emergency in a number of the country's public housing developments. It was the eleventh month in a row that the Swedish Air Force—along with the French, Americans, and others—was bombing the last remnants of Daesh in Syria, ISIS, and that summer there were terrorist attacks in Berlin, Toulouse, and London, the first executed by a group of right-wing extremists, the latter two by people who claimed to be connected to Daesh.

I looked up from the papers and caught my reflection in the bus window, a transparent mask floating over the spruce trees and road signs.

I worried about my country.

That night when I told Isra about the meeting, something remained unsaid. I couldn't find the words. Isra flipped through the girl's pages and dismissed the account, more or less, as paranoid fantasies, and when I told her that the girl had said she came from the Rabbit Yard, the same public housing development in Gothenburg I had grown up in, she simply took it as a sign that the girl was trying to manipulate me and that nothing about our meeting had been innocent.

We sat on the sofa; I was watching the news on my laptop; our daughter was sleeping in my arms; outside, the autumn rain was finally turning to snow.

"What aren't you telling me?"

"She has something about her," I said. "Something just outside my field of vision." My daughter's fingers gently scratched my arm and the wrinkled domes of her eyelids quivered in the screen's bluish green light. I stroked her hair. Something about the girl in the clinic, something I sensed like an echo or a shadow, frightened me so much it made my hands shake.

I'm writing to those of you who can't sleep either. Every time I close my eyes, I straight up get the feeling that they're searching the halls, and they'll soon find me. People who wish me harm.

I'm writing to those of you who have also spent hours staring at shadows on the ceiling.

Sometimes I could catch some sleep on buses and streetcars.

Wallah, I used to nod off on the back of Amin's moped.

All this is about him, but not like you think.

I have a small window in my room here. I sit up. Sometimes I see snow and rain or leaves blowing off the trees. One of the lights in the rec yard is right under my window and it makes everything that falls through the night shine as though dipped in silver.

I run to the fence, jump up, and climb. As I'm hurling myself over, my parka snags and the padding comes out in a tangle of long white cotton intestines. I land on the other side. Behind me I hear guard dogs barking. I tear off my jacket, and that's when I remember Liat, because she had given it to me years ago. A black parka with a hood and a fur trim, an American knockoff.

My mother once said that history is a memory that flashes through your mind when you're running for your life, and as I'm running from the Rabbit Yard, over gravel and stubbly grass, I remember the playground in our yard and the swings where we used to sit.

There's an old shopping mall ahead, towering in the night like a fortress. I know it. It was built when I was a newborn but no one went there. Crawling in through a broken shop window, I get cut by the glass. I make my way up an escalator and run past rusty, graffitied shutters and cement pillars. *Death to Islam. Amin = All Muslims.* I've been here with Liat; I know my way. I crawl into a clothing store, in among fallen mannequins, curl up, and listen to the barking dogs.

A carpet over a balcony railing beating in the wind. The empty swing between us rocked slowly.

Let me start with Liat instead.

Start with love.

I chugged my energy drink and threw the can in the sand.

Let me start with the ordinary, because that's where the madness is.

We sat in the same swings we'd sat in as children. It was one of the first days after summer vacation, but we were already ditching school.

Liat had freckles but was dark-haired like me; she was shorter than me, but her shoulders were broader. She'd gotten them from handball. Earbuds in, one hand drumming her thigh. We were crazy about this one pop star called Oh Nana Yurg. We copied her hairstyles and bought knockoffs of the designer clothing she wore in her videos, wishing she'd come pick us up in her helicopter.

The empty swing rocked, the rug flapped in the wind. I leaned back, gained speed. If you looked past the playground's rusty jungle gym and beyond the apartment blocks you'd have seen a bus shelter, but instead of an ad, on the side a video would be playing on an LCD screen. That was normal. Where I come from, those panels playing the video are everywhere.

The video was a little choppy and pixilated where people had thrown stones at the glass or kicked it. The important thing wasn't that a video was playing at a bus stop, yani, but *which* video was playing: the same one I recorded during our attack.

The video about him.

It was an average day in the place where I came from, the place I finally remembered in the comic book store, and there, in that world, it wasn't me who had filmed those events, but Amin's sister, Nour. She didn't die when they were little; she'd grown up with Amin.

Liat took the earbuds out.

"Huh?"

"I didn't say anything," I said. She spit in the sand. Oh Nana Yurg's latest track was buzzing and rattling in the earbuds that hung from a neon yellow cord around her neck. "So did your mom sign it this year?"

Liat nodded. On the flickering display out in the dust and sunshine, Amin was grabbing hold of Loberg's hair and pulling his head backward, but right before he slit his throat, the video clip cut and a line of text appeared, white on black:

It all could have been different.

What came next was information about the so-called "citizen contract": an electronic document that every adult in the place I'm from had to sign when they filed their taxes each spring and then again in the fall. Some people refused to sign and they became something called an "Enemy of Sweden"—yani Muslims and Jews and other, like, extremists—and ended up in a place called the Rabbit Yard. Whoosh. Gone.

In my hands, the swing's chains were cold.

I'm only writing this now.

I come from a place where Amin did kill that artist, and where his sister detonated her bomb vest when the police tried to enter the store. They got everything on video.

I don't remember what year I come from. When I was on that swing, the iWatch 9 had just been released, and Oh Nana Yurg had dropped a new playlist with a BDSM theme, but none of this means anything here, in your world. I also know that I was in my third year of high school and I was one year old when the attack on Hondo's happened, and so I must come from somewhere fifteen years in a future.

I leaned back in the swing and opened my eyes, saw the world upside down, the playground, all those windows reflecting the clouds. You know, my social studies teacher out there in the fucking future used to be all, "How about you share something with us about sharia law," and "How about you tell us a little bit about the difference between Shia and Sunni Muslims," and "How about…?"

What a loser.

"Mom probably isn't gonna sign this year," I said and shut my eyes.

"*Balagan*," Liat said, and if you don't know that word, it means crash, yani, chaos.

Leaking from the earbuds around Liat's neck, Oh Nana Yurg's voice was rough and paper-thin. It was a song about chasing this one thing from Shinjuku to Beijing, and back then I thought that thing must be happiness—wallah, what a baby—later we got that it was about this one drug that made it impossible for you to say no—she wanted to get some and give it to a special guy.

I felt the blood flowing through my upside-down head and it pounded dully and kinda creepily, but I laid there and echoed:

"Total balagan, yo."

Liat's father was already an enemy of Sweden but not because he'd refused to sign the citizen contract. He'd smuggled illegal meat into the country. Her family wasn't actually strict about stuff like that, but that spring he wanted them to have a real Passover and got caught near Öresund with a frozen lamb shank in his trunk. He and Liat's mom had been divorced for years, and Liat didn't really know him. I guess that's why he'd tried to hook up the lamb. To give her something of himself. Same difference, though: him being in the Rabbit Yard now or him being in that apartment he used to have across town.

Real talk, it was still balagan for her.

I started to feel sick and sat up. She ran her fingers through her hair, trying to get a tangle out—this was when she was still climbing up balconies, stabbing people in the eye with scissors, before she realized the danger that was inside her, too, like with guys and stuff—and over at the bus stop Amin was raising the box cutter, the screen went black, and that text popped up again:

It all could have been different.

Mom put out a ceramic dish of incense on the coffee table. I remember that dish exactly, the blue and green floral pattern and each hairline crack in the glaze. Mom bought it on a pilgrimage to Mecca, before it was illegal to go. The smoke rose to the ceiling, I sat on the sofa in front of the window and ran my hand through it to make it twirl into tiny clouds. Mom sat next to me. I don't remember her name. I don't remember where in Gothenburg we lived or what she did for a living.

"Would you like to go to Algeria?"

"On vacation?" I asked. That's where she was from, and we'd visited when I was little, but that was years ago. The willow tree outside moved in the wind, the slim leaves rustling like metal strips.

"On a trip," Mom said. She was Sufi, yani a mystic, and I remember her sitting awake all night meditating by whispering God's ninety-nine names again and again. Wallah, a Jedi knight.

"When?"

"We have to save up for it. Next winter, maybe?"

I don't remember the color of her eyes. I do remember the fading henna tattoo on her hands, which I'd applied the week before.

Dad was cooking in the kitchen, he heard us talking and called out:

"If you don't sign they'll freeze our bank account."

Mom didn't reply. I couldn't tell if Dad was joking or serious. The citizen contract was usually something faraway that had nothing to do with my life, something that belonged to the world we learned about in school, yani government and districts and Swedish values and stuff, but still, sometimes it was like central to everything, central to each ordinary moment.

"Are you really not going to sign?" I asked.

"I don't know, darling."

A flutter of sparrows swarmed and landed in the willow tree. There's something doubled about my childhood, a feeling that I wasn't who I thought I was. I remember wanting to change my name to Hedvig or Elsa, names that seemed to belong to the ground beneath my feet and the blue sky above.

I imagined switching bodies with Liat, of course to get her muscular arms and those eyes that narrowed into slits when she smiled or got angry, but also to get her courage.

"I don't know," Mom repeated. This was the day she first started talking about fleeing to Algeria, but I didn't really get that then.

I remember her watching the sparrows, saying that they were gathering for evening prayer. Their habit of arriving in a twirling cloud and making a racket was how they praised God.

Dancing by myself in the storm of light from a disco ball, spinning with my arms out like a cross. #Houseparty. Liat's older brother had gone to the liquor store for us and I raised the bottle and took a drink, and it was like *I* was still and the parquet floor and house were spinning around me, faster and faster, and then I threw up a transparent mess that splashed on my feet and someone shouted, "You nasty Muslim, learn to hold your fucking liquor."

Balagan.

The way we used to chase down happiness.

I remember the reflections of light sliding across my half-digested food.

Two Swedish girls followed me out into the garden; they had gold makeup around their eyes and I thought they were angels because they held my hair while I vomited. I remember the grass under my wet socks, the throb of music through the walls. Do you think the conflict between Sunni Muslims and Shia Muslims can be resolved peacefully? Does your dad make you wear such big pants or did you pick them out yourself? Do you think people should be allowed to vote if they don't have Swedish values?

After a while the two girls left, and I sat on the lawn with my head in my hands. I was chasing something from Shinjuku to Beijing. Maybe it was God. I started laughing. A joke I'd heard by the lockers in school that day. Why can't the peace force defeat the terrorists? Because they don't have access to the latest weapons of mass destruction: immigrants, those illiterate welfare cases that multiply like #rats.

The space where we went to pray was quiet and damp, located on the ground floor of a twelve-story building. The ceiling was inlaid with large ventilation ducts made of mottled gray aluminum. Isra and our daughter went into the women's area, and I slowly washed my drained face.

During the sermon I looked out the window, at the apartment blocks across the way.

I'd come to the Rabbit Yard to go to Friday prayer, but also to take stock of something in the girl from Tundra's story. I wanted to hold what she'd asserted about this place up to the light of something tangible and see what gave way.

Now and then a bicycle or moped passed by outside.

Mom arrived from Gambia alone and moved here after spending a few months at a refugee camp outside of Helsingborg. She met Dad, a Swedish social-work student, at a nightclub, and they were both a bit rootless. They got married before I was born, but divorced when I was just a few years old and my sister was a newborn. Dad moved to Uppsala, where he still lives, and I grew up here, in the Rabbit Yard with Mom.

The imam holding the day's sermon was only a few years

older than I was. He seemed about to be swallowed by his baggy outfit made of a patterned fabric with a waxy shine. He spoke about Daesh, about the leaders who were recruiting our children to die in their increasingly hopeless war, in a *jihad* that didn't annihilate the "self" in humanity, but rather the "other."

"Where are their own children? Are they blowing themselves up to get to paradise?" he said—West African, sinewy but broad shouldered, wearing a small crocheted cap called a kufi on his head. "No. They're studying in England, in the United States," he looked at us, one by one, allowing the thought to sink in. "As our young people die."

I recognized a few of the men from my youth: brothers of classmates, faces from nights within dreams about flying or falling.

I pressed my forehead to the mat. Submission, the feeling of rushing water, liberation from myself.

A ragged soccer ball spun through the rising dust and seemed to hang in the air—a gray moon that for a moment eclipsed the sun. We were sitting on a park bench on the square, I'd brought cookies with me, our daughter ate a couple and then we fed the rest to the pigeons.

"You're thinking about her," said Isra. "The girl at the clinic."

I looked at the people moving through the cool, clear air of the square, running their errands, with their worries and cares.

"Why would she make up a story about a world where she never stopped Amin?" I asked. "And why would she say she was from here? From the Rabbit Yard?"

Isra is from Algeria, like the mother in the girl's

account—the girl must have read about her in one of my books and used that detail to connect with me. Like with the Rabbit Yard. But why had she reached out to me in the first place? I sensed darkness again, the feeling of a threat just beyond my peripheral vision.

I searched for the window where I'd lived with my mom but couldn't find it. Together with the Fox Yard and the Sparrow Yard, the tall apartment blocks sinking into the violet afternoon light matched the bigger public housing projects in nearby Biskopsgården and Länsmansgården. The area had been constructed in the early sixties. As far as I know the names were plucked out of thin air—there were no more rabbits here than anywhere else.

Many of the people I grew up with had long since left. They were behind bars or lost to drugs. One friend got shot when we were seventeen, which was a sort of breaking point for me. Some simply moved away. Did we become birds? Why that image? The terrible freedom, that's all, of never having been wanted here. One buddy went to Syria and joined a jihadist group, and I thought about him as I scanned the hundreds of identical windows. I was remembering his laugh, bold and boundless, and how as children we'd run around these buildings, through the lobbies and into basements, sneaking cigarettes, stealing bicycles, and swapping CDs of New York rap with each other. He turned up on the front pages a few years before the attack. He came from these streets, like me. Somalian. Swedish. These streets with no end. The Rabbit Yard.

My daughter poured a handful of cookie crumbs out of the bag and passed from sight, laughing from within a tempest of wings.

This was the spring after I first visited the clinic.

I know you know about insomnia because you write about it. I like your books, they remind me of people tightrope-walking, high up in the air. They're made beautiful by fear, you know?

I know everything about fear.

When I woke up in the hospital I had it, fear, but it didn't really have a target. When I was with Amin, in the days and nights we shared before the attack, I was afraid of losing him, because he was the only person I could remember. Then, in the middle of the chaos at Hondo's, when everything came back to me, I wasn't afraid anymore, because I believed that everything that could happen to me had already happened.

Now, as I sit awake at night trying to figure out what to write to you, I feel afraid again.

Liat and I headed home, past the ethanol station's cracked sign, a yellow glow under the September sky.

"Have you heard from your dad?"

"Yo, cellphones and shit don't work in the Rabbit Yard," she said. We stopped on a footbridge, she cleared her throat and let the wind stretch the loogie dangling from her lip into a silver thread.

Top five crazy-ass things Liat's done in her life. Number five: filming the boys locker room and posting it online in middle school. Four: in elementary school she ate an entire glue stick; had to go to the hospital and everything.

"Mom ended up signing it," I said. I remember the sky was streaked with contrails that day, like hashmarks etched on a pane of glass. "You know we're going to Algeria, right? I mean, like...moving."

The loogie dropped from Liat's lip and left a white snail-trail on the roof of a moving car.

"Say wallah."

"Wallah," I said, and wanted to say more but I didn't have the words.

Number three was easy. The first boy she'd kissed, and back when she'd only ever kissed one boy, went around talking smack about her after, so she hit him with a hockey stick and split his lip. Hospitals and everything. She said:

"Israel was wack cuz everybody thought I was a *suedi* there."

"Like, what you eat and stuff?"

"Exactly."

The same thing had happened to me in Algeria.

Two: She got locked out once, like in third grade, and was trying to climb over to her apartment from one of her neighbor's balconies, but got stuck and was left dangling from a railing on the fourth floor. The fire department had to use a ladder to get her down. Number one was a no-brainer, too: In eighth grade she threw a pair of scissors at Omar because he'd started in on her about being Jewish and me being a traitor for being her best friend, and they hit him in the eye. The scissors got stuck in his face like a ninja star. Hospitals and everything.

"When are you going?"

"Next year, I think. We gotta get the cash together first."

Sometimes even I told jokes about Muslims. I told them to Liat or other kids hanging outside the mall to put some distance between me and the images, to prove I wasn't like Amin.

"So a suicide bomber gets to paradise," I said, "and all of the seventy-two virgins have beards just like him." The suedis indulged me, blowing smoke at the cool sunlight.

I could talk about my dad's childhood, and it would be like your story about having a parent who sometimes wished she'd stayed across the sea. I could mention that he had diabetes but still ate a bag of rosewater Turkish Delight every Saturday, while he and Mom watched their web series. I could describe his hands, those long slender fingers of his.

But most of all he was a person who wrote, I think, but he kept it secret from me for a long time, even though I'm not really sure why. I only knew then that he was always reading: in nearly every memory he's bent over a book and only looks up at me briefly, almost frightened. Like he thinks what's happening on that page will keep going without him.

I always stayed in the doorway.

I guess he liked books because they allowed him to be someone else.

"What's that one about?" I asked one day. The book open on the desk was yellow and used, dog-eared and covered in someone else's notes, and I'm guessing it was one of the books that had been banned by the so-called February Laws—the same laws that governed the citizen contract and what was happening in the Rabbit Yard—because the cover had been torn off. He said:

"It's about how the world's poor will one day secure their freedom."

"Dad?"

"Yes?"

I wanted to tell him that something was happening to me, something I didn't understand. I leaned against the doorframe.

Did you hear the one about the Muslim who became prime minister? Did you hear the one about the Muslim who wanted to fly?

In the act of writing, I've noticed, there is a loneliness that reminds me of how when telling jokes you can abandon everything, even yourself.

"You know Amin?"

"The terrorist?"

I nodded, said: "I dreamed about him last night."

"No surprise there," Dad mumbled, never taking his eyes from the page. "With them showing his face all over." He wrote something down next to one of the existing notes and flipped through the book.

In your time, you still have paper books everywhere, but where I come from it was super weird to be sitting around flipping through a real book. It's like, people thought you were a refugee. And Dad had a ton of banned books. He hid them under his mattress, and slept on them, which made him seem even weirder to me.

In my dreams, which I'd started having that fall, and which I wanted to talk to him about, Amin looked at me and said, "Light."

That night I started an account on Sensly, which was an app, sort of like the Facebook you have in your time, Mom and Dad even used it sometimes, but you didn't post videos, you wrote. Putting your feelings out there in short posts for others to heart or hate. Yani *sensitive*. Curled up in bed with my cellphone, I wanted to write something true and important, but all it ended up being was a list of Oh Nana Yurg's best lyrics. I remember getting up and looking out the window, and seeing the swings moving in the wind, and it reminded me of a chorus in a song she'd released a long time ago, and I put it at the top of the list.

We're just a bubble floating in the glass of God's breath.

A bubble in God's breath.

I scrolled around for a nice selfie, changed my mind, and looked for a picture of a Swedish girl instead. I didn't pick the most extra one, you know: a blond with braids in a folk costume, like certain politicians were wearing in parliament. Just a Swede.

This is the first time I'm telling anyone this.

I pretended to have a different face.

Liat met someone and dropped off the radar that winter, and I posted on Sensly about BFFs who betray each other and about the freezing sparrows flocking in the willow tree. I rarely wrote about God, and never about being Muslim or that my best friend was Jewish and her dad was in the Rabbit Yard.

I started reading the books on dad's bookshelves. I learned to like their weight and the rough touch of the pages. I was drawn to poetry, which could compress the world into a single Sensly line. One of my favorite poems was written by a blind Iranian poet. It was about how her blindness made her helpless against men who pulled her into the dark, but one day her blindness protected her from the brightness of bombs being dropped on the city where she lived. What I actually liked the most was how she imagined everything she couldn't see—yani beauty, like fall colors, which she referred to as gold tossed into a grave, wasted, or how the shadows under trees went white with frost, as if the grass were the hair of summer aging.

It was like she could see better because she was blind.

I thought about words that winter. Like "Swedish." You were Swedish if the Swedes thought you were Swedish—that's what we learned in our Core Values class. I wasn't Swedish because I was Muslim or whatever. But I mean, who was the first Swede anyway—the one who'd decided who got to be Swedish? He didn't exist, and there was a hole where he was supposed to be, a hole inside the word "Swedish" that sometimes made it look like the faces of my laughing classmates were masks cut out of plastic or paper.

An emptiness.

I sat in the living room window thinking. I missed Liat. We met up a few times when our class schedules lined up, but she was quiet and depressed. Balagan. #boytrouble.

Dad took me downtown one night. As usual he was sunk into himself, even sitting next to me on the bus, shadows flitting across his face. I asked him where we were going, and that's when he told me. He'd noticed I was reading a lot of poetry. Did I know that he wrote poetry himself sometimes, and once his poetry had been published in books? I felt a pang of loneliness when I realized he must have gotten Mom to help him keep that secret from me my entire childhood, and I remember the words he used to brush it all off, "It was another time."

We got off and walked to a venue with white walls and furniture made of polished metal. Piles of glossy magazines were lying around. A year ago, Oh Nana Yurg had been photographed for one of them, and Liat and I had drooled over the issue in a store window, so I knew the magazines were about fashion and art and were sometimes printed with real gold leaf and each issue cost, like, as much as a month's rent in our neighborhood.

When Dad introduced me, the people in the venue hugged me like I was their long-lost daughter, and I understood they were part of Dad's former life, when he'd published books and was maybe even Swedish.

Eventually the reading began, which didn't sound at all like the poems in the books Dad had at home, but more like a code, or like drunks on the bus mumbling to themselves, repeating the same sentence over and over again but never getting anywhere. I could tell that this was how the poets were trying to point out the emptiness in the words.

When Dad took a piece of paper from his jacket pocket and walked to the stage, which really was no more than a raised part of the white floor, the audience laughed because he wasn't reading from a tablet or a cellphone—wallah senior citizen.

I remember the clean white wall behind him, how it seemed to swallow him, and his trembling hands made the paper rustle like dry leaves. I associated his nerves with the expensive magazines, the color white, and how people were dressed.

He read a poem about stones that melted because they bore a light that he related to sharia, the law, and the audience fidgeted anxiously and many looked disappointed when he said the Arabic word. A few slipped out to smoke. He didn't notice what was happening. I remember the weakness I perceived in his smile on the bus ride home.

During physics the next week, our teacher created emptiness in a glass tube using a vacuum pump, and I panicked because I imagined the glass was going to blow up and unleash that emptiness. I got up from my seat and bolted from the school.

It was the summer of gold caps and Soulland sweatshirts, the summer the iWatch 12 came out and Oh Nana Yurg released an album with a cover photo of her dressed as a soldier with night-vision goggles and a tight black stealth outfit.

The morning of one of the first days of summer vacation, Dad was kneeling in the living room, bent over his cupped hands, whispering a prayer into them. The window was open, the curtains were rippling, and I remember his hands and thinking that it was like he was trying to protect something small and fragile from a storm.

That summer Liat reappeared, as suddenly as she had disappeared, and we hung out on the roof of the parking structure, tanning and smoking.

"I mean, smoking used to be legal."

"That's crazy, cuz," she said.

"Hella crazy. That's what I'm saying. Balagan."

Liat took a drag of my cigarette.

"My mom used to smoke a pack a day when we moved here from Israel."

She'd broken up with her boyfriend, who hadn't allowed her to see anyone else, wallah #stalker, and her new one, Bilal, was sitting on the edge, and he had his long, muscular arms around her waist. His dad was from Senegal and he had a Swedish mom, did MMA—yani mixed martial arts, in case you know what that is—but I thought he seemed fragile, with those cauliflower ears of his sticking out and his glittering black eyes that were like two drops of a clear and starry sky. I liked him because he didn't say much, was older, and had a car.

Liat asked what was up with Algeria and I said we'd probably go in the fall, but we still didn't have the cash. Liat offered Bilal the cigarette over her shoulder so he could smoke without letting go of her. He started coughing. He was only smoking because of her. It made me dizzy seeing them sitting there, so close to the edge, high above the dry lawns and speed bumps and roundabouts. Liat leaned her head against Bilal's chest and shut her eyes against the sun.

"Yo," she said. "Let's go to the Rabbit Yard."

It might sound crazy to you that people ended up in a camp because they hadn't signed their contracts or had eaten kosher or halal, and that my best friend's dad was there. But for us it was normal. We crossed the bridge in Bilal's rusty car; we blew smoke out the windows and blasted Oh Nana Yurg—Bilal let us even though he thought it was kid's music. After we passed the last bus stop Liat's eyes went dark.

We drove through an industrial area, past piles of roofing tiles and gas-powered cars that had rusted away, and then past the empty shopping center. In pink letters that stood several meters high on the roof, it said *Mål of Gothenburg*.

As we approached the tall fence topped with rolls of razor wire, Bilal turned off the stereo.

When Amin and I were rolling around on his 180 or messing around in random apartment buildings, before we met Hamad, we sometimes ended up at the Rabbit Yard. Amin dealt, yani selling hash and speed and blow and stuff back then. You've probably read about it in the papers, our life together. And the thing is that sometimes when we crossed an empty square out in the Rabbit Yard, with our hoods up against the wind, I'd get the sickest feeling that I'd been there before and start shivering like I was freezing, and the hair on my neck would stand on end, and I'd say to Amin that it was like I was walking over my own grave or visiting the place where I'd die.

I no longer think time is a straight line. I don't think this story or any other story a person can tell has one single beginning, but several. And nothing ever really ends.

In the world I come from, what happened was that there'd been chaos in the Rabbit Yard, shootings and car fires and stuff, balagan, and mold was found in lots of the buildings too, so eventually the politicians cleared the people out and the buildings stood empty, but then a company started putting refugees in them, and then after all the refugees were deported, it became one of the places where the enemies of Sweden were sent.

A pair of crows circled the buildings. Lots of the balconies had rusted to pieces, and you could see right through a crumbled wall. In one of the apartments a woman wearing a niqab was praying.

Liat was clutching the fence, staring at something, and Bilal killed time shadowboxing by the car, short, tight blows, spinning, kicking, feinting.

I remember Liat's hair in the wind, her just standing there, completely still.

A security guard's car pulled up, probably thinking we were there to help someone escape. The guards started fucking with us—"Show us your passports" and stuff—two young pimply suedis, and Liat perked up, fucking with them back and she even pushed one of them. I think she hoped Bilal would wail on them. But Bilal said, "Chill baby chill."

In my time, you could download an app that checked a passport number against a registry of enemies of Sweden, and according to the February Laws citizens were allowed to screen each other. On top of that there were some mobile games that were all about reporting enemies of Sweden, so we "non-Swedes" always carried our passports, and it was, like, no problem—the guards typed our passport numbers into their cellphones and then told us to go home.

"Tell me about God."

"What do you want to hear?"

Mom and me, sitting across from each other on the sofa. I said: "A story from when I was little. When I couldn't sleep."

"The first thing God created was a pen."

"A pen?"

She nodded and a smile lit up her face, like when the wind plasters a leaf to the window and the sun shines through it and you see every rib and vein.

Yani, you could see her soul.

"A pen, alone in the dark," she said. "And it asked God what he wanted to write."

"What did God say?"

"Write down everything that's going to happen from now until the end of time."

"Is that what the pen did?"

"Yes," she said and touched my neck in her tender, distracted way. "That was the beginning of everything. A pen, describing this. Me being here, and you, and us touching each other. The grains of sand changing color as the sun moves across the beaches in Algeria. The past and future."

I know you don't believe me, but I'm writing to you anyway, because I have to tell somebody.

I'm writing to you who once wrote that fear was like powder in the air when you were growing up, it got in your hair and eyes and you breathed it in.

I don't remember how many men were pushing their way through the mall, just that it felt like there were more of them than there were of us. I waited for Liat by the exit, thinking at first that it had something to do with soccer or a student prank. A man with steel-rimmed glasses was handing out flyers and a few people with their arms around each other's shoulders were singing a booming, kinda melancholic song but I couldn't catch the words. Some of the men in the group heading my direction were my age, others were older than Dad, all of them were wearing dark jackets and the occasional Swedish flag worn like a cape, streaked with soot where the fabric had dragged across the ground. A few had blue-and-yellow strips of fabric tied over their faces, and a pudgy, bald salesman type had a sword slung over his shoulder—I mean a real sword like in the Middle Ages, like something out of a museum, unwieldy and with a dull blade.

One of them kicked a panhandler's cup. The money scattered across the dirty mall floor. A few coins landed at my feet, and in the sunlight spilling through the mall's glass doors they were like drops of white-hot metal. The beggar started picking them up, but the man poked him with his sword from behind pretty hard, making him lose his balance and fall to his belly. The men laughed and I remember the taste of iron in my mouth, my skin was sticky with sweat. I'd later find out that the men called themselves Crusading Hearts, a name they'd taken from the warriors that had seized Jerusalem from the Muslims. On the flyers they were handing out, Amin's face was crossed out in blue.

Mom corrected my Arabic pronunciation when I tried to say, "I'm from Sweden, nice to meet you." My Arabic was better when I was little, before I started preschool. I looked out the living room window, at the willow tree, the leaves of which had wilted into dragon scales, and wondered if it had always been my fate to have my life split between two places, one where they couldn't pronounce my last name and the other where I couldn't speak with the people in their own tongue. I thought about Algeria more often, about the lemon groves by the sea, which I remembered from my visit as a child—their smell reminding me of dishwashing liquid and chewing gum.

Mom said: "*Ahlan wa sahlan.*"

For me the lemon trees were connected with the people of Algeria, the people who in my memory leaned against white-washed walls, unhappy and somehow unreal, and that, like me, were forever waiting for nothing.

I said: "*Allan va sallan.*"

I wrote on Sensly every night, mostly love poems. I called myself Agnes, after a girl in my class, and people commented and clicked the heart and told me to keep fighting when I was feeling down. They wrote that I seemed like a good person and that I wrote so well about what growing up was like. Some people wanted to meet IRL and asked if I actually lived in Gothenburg.

I got something out of it.

Me, Liat, and Bilal went back to the Rabbit Yard sometimes. It was the summer we started exploring the Mål of Gothenburg: breaking into stores and rooting around in the clothes and empty boxes. Bilal found a pair of sneakers, a few sizes too big, but he kept them anyway. Often he and Liat went off on their own and I sat there in the dark, waiting.

Sometimes I fantasized about being able to meet Amin, like, what I'd say to him. You know:

"Why'd you do it?"

"For your sake," he'd reply. "Because of what they did to you."

When we started school, the halls were buzzing with rumors about the Crusading Hearts. A girl in my class had an older brother who was a Crusading Heart and she said that he was part of some sort of militia and had a gun that he practiced shooting over the sea. I listened along with my classmates and felt my life being diverted away from them, like a stream of rainwater dragging a few blades of grass with it, swirling down into a storm drain.

Did you hear the one about the Muslim who was shopping for a car? Why don't Jews or Muslims eat pork? What do you call a Muslim who can swim? Did you hear the one about the Muslim who met the pope?

Liat broke up with Bilal, maybe because he never really ripped on the guards who kept chasing us away from the Rabbit Yard. Instead she got together with a dude in our class named Martin, a Swede.

Once, when Liat and I were talking on the swings, Bilal showed up. He was crying and saying he wanted her back, he'd do anything, and she kissed him goodbye one last time. I remember them holding each other, wound together against his car that magnetic fall night.

Over at the bus shelter they've begun showing that video with Amin again, because yet again it was time to sign the citizen contract.

We looked at each other.

"They're pitting us all against each other. You're either an enemy or a friend."

"No, I'm afraid it's worse than that," Mom said. There was something in Mom and Dad's voices when they talked in the kitchen in the evenings: fear pulsed beneath their words. "You're either human or an animal." I remember praying with them later, and how the traces our hands left on the prayer mats resembled feathers.

One night I saw a man on the bus wearing a real knight's helmet. He was wasted and stumbling around and screaming about Muslims as was to be expected, about how we were all going to die or whatever. He might have been, like, a physics or history teacher. Swaying from the helmet was a red plume.

"They're giving me cancer," he screamed, and I rested my forehead against the frosty window and pretended he wasn't talking about me, and thought about how the events I'd witnessed growing up were like a force in search of the lowest common denominator in people, which it wanted to harness, and then put to its own use.

The frozen image on the laptop screen seemed to vibrate. I'd spent hours watching the video from Hondo's, playing it, replaying it. Right where I had paused it, Amin looked starved. The balaclava was pulled up to his forehead. Behind him was a shelf full of comics and a small stain on Hondo's shop window.

The girl who'd written the mysterious story about the future—by this point I'd read the story at least twenty times—had been his wife and must have loved him.

Isra sat down with me at the desk and rested her chin in her hand.

"Are you going back?"

"To Tundra? Why?"

"So you can get answers to your questions. To find out why she contacted you; hear the rest of her story."

I didn't reply. Isra reached out and touched the screen, unexpectedly, lingering.

"You know what this picture reminds me of?" she said. I shook my head. "Those photographs of soldiers from before and after war. Remember them?"

I nodded. The photo series had turned up on social media.

Portraits of Swedish soldiers. The first pictures were taken before they traveled to the newly opened fronts of the war on terror, in Yemen and West Africa, and elsewhere. More pictures were taken while the men and women were in the throes of war. Then, pictures were taken after. The aim was clear: to show the impact of war on a human face—when the soldiers returned to Sweden they had an extinguished and somehow sullied look in their eyes. Isra and I had talked about it because she'd discussed the photographs in an academic paper she was writing at the time. What had maybe been more shocking to us than seeing the entropy of war at work was how their faces looked so strangely alive in the portraits taken during combat, as if they were in a hypervigilant state, run through with something that resembles joy.

We sat in front of the screen. I wasn't able to say that I was wondering if we too had been drawn into a war. A war that was a measure of speed, a war where skin—or something more diffuse, something called "Swedishness"—was the uniform.

Amin's face was pale and the shadows made it look inhospitable and sharp. A landscape of white cliffs. The tense mouth. His hand blurred by movement.

A spectral war, a war that, in a terrible way, was made up of images of the dying and the dead.

A war on what was war and what was peace.

Flashes of blue light in those large, dark eye sockets.

Daesh believed themselves to be in a war with the entire world. They thought they were fighting a war that would call angels down to earth. Literally speaking, a war that would annihilate creation.

Did I want to return to Tundra? I scratched my beard, shut my eyes tight. Which of my questions did I think a locked up, schizophrenic girl could answer?

That night I spent a long time looking at our daughter's face as she slept. I swept back the fever-wet curls plastered to her chin. She writhed in her sleep, inside some vision that responded to my touch. Her face, I knew, was as endless as paradise.

Maybe the pictures were only like that because the soldiers had been photographed deep inside a dense and all-penetrating desert light.

Maybe violence had been emptied of emptiness too.

On June nineteenth, an unknown man shot up the prayer hall I visited in the Rabbit Yard. A sixteen-year-old died, several people were injured. A minute of silence for the victims was held at his school but no greater interest was shown by the media or governmental bodies; it was assumed that the shooting was related to the dead's connection to certain gangs. It was one of many fatal shootings in the Rabbit Yard that year. Like many Muslims in Gothenburg, I visited prayer halls. A few days had passed, but surprisingly enough, two police were posted by the broken basement window: apparently someone, possibly the murderer, had thrown a hand grenade through the window during the night. A young guy who'd been praying next to me mentioned it on our way out the door—nothing was in the news.

I remember the bullet holes in the windowpanes. They were like craters in the lunar landscape that had been expanding between me and my country during these years.

That evening, an anonymous blogger claimed the deed. He described the ammunition that had been used, which the police interpreted as proof that he, in all likelihood, was the murderer. The blogger turned out to be a white Swede, motivated by racism. He wasn't called a terrorist by the media, because then Swedish families would have to be bugged, monitored, and harassed.

I returned to the place again a couple of days later, not really knowing why. People who'd visited the prayer hall after the blog post, anti-racists mainly, had stuck flowers through the bullet holes in the window, echoing a gesture from the attack on Hondo's—where people had stuck white roses through the bullet holes in the store window the following morning. I wanted to go in and pray, as though to reestablish something holy, but the door was locked.

The feeling of theater, unreality.

One night during a grocery store run with my daughter, she looked up at the stars that had appeared high above us and asked why they existed, and I said they were there so travelers could find their way home in the dark. Then I thought about the girl from Tundra, about her story, I thought I understood her desire to transform the events we'd both been witnessing for years from a descent into the abyss to exactly what I was telling my daughter about: a way home.

3

The doctor was a Swedish man, a little younger than me. We were alone in the visiting room: he shook my hand without getting up, asked me if I'd had a good journey, and said something about the weather, about lingering thunder; and then he asked if I'd read her account and what my thoughts were, as an author. From where I was sitting, I couldn't tell if he was observing me or looking out the window—his glasses reflected the room's bare walls, the halogen lights on the ceiling, the small rectangular window's armored glass.

"I don't really know," I said. "But I'd say that she's done some writing before."

"That was my assessment too," he said. He was wearing a black T-shirt with the name of what I assumed was a hard rock band written in barbed wire across his chest, and distressed jeans—clothing that sharply contrasted with his mannerisms. I would've guessed his family was upper class; he had an alarm unit on his belt.

"Has she had any visitors besides me?"

"Her mother's been here twice, once with her brother."

"From Belgium?" I asked. His hands were clasped over his belly and he nodded slowly. He had a sort of measured arrogance about him.

"But, as noted, she doesn't believe they're related."

"This idea that she's from the future," I said, "how does she think she ended up here, in our time?"

He studied his watch with a pout.

"We don't know. In fact we've never been able to come as close to understanding her imagined world as when she wrote you."

I sensed I was part of a power struggle between him and someone else; I could only guess at the contours of the conflict, but in one way or another it must've been about who the patients opened up to.

"Of course we monitor the inmates' activity on the library computers," he said. "Why do you want to see her again?"

"I might write about her."

"A book?"

"Maybe an article," I said.

She turned up eventually, accompanied by a guard. She was thinner than when I'd last seen her; she seemed drained: dull skin, dark rings under her eyes.

"As-salaamu-alaikum."

"*Wa-alaikum-as-salaam*," I replied, more out of reflex than anything else; I still felt the same about her using those words to greet me. I pressed record and put my cellphone on the table. She went over to the window. The view must've been different than from the other rooms she had access to. She was holding a bunch of papers, folded lengthwise, and I scolded myself for the prick of joy I felt when I saw them.

"Can I ask you something?"

"Isn't that why you're here?"

"What landed you here, with us? In the past?"

The window was reinforced with chicken wire enmeshed

in the glass and she followed one of the thin threads with her finger.

"I mean, for me this isn't the past. When I traveled back in time I didn't arrive in the history of my world, but in a different history, you see what I mean?"

I decided to keep playing along, since I'd already committed, and said:

"Where you grew up, in your future, Amin's sister participated in the attack against Hondo's. But in our world she died in an accident in a bathtub when she was little."

She turned around, glanced at the doctor, a smile passing over her lips, possibly with a touch of mocking hostility.

"You all think I'm crazy," she said. I would've responded that I thought she was sick and needed help, and I waited for the doctor to say something along those lines, but he didn't, so I said:

"You wrote something about time."

"I don't think time is a line."

"So what is it then?"

"I don't know," she said. "A landscape."

"But how did you get here? To our time, our world?"

"I'll try to write about it. It was like..." She interrupted herself, her eyelids fluttered. "I was in that comic book store looking down at my phone. And it was like waking up and finding my entire real life inside it. I knew I'd already seen what I was filming at least a thousand times before."

"Because it was used by the fascists in the Sweden you come from?"

"I don't know what that word means. *Fajists.*" She mispronounced the word, but I didn't bother to correct her.

"It means people who follow a certain ideology."

"We didn't have that word," she said. "Or, like, maybe

Mom and Dad knew it, but I never heard it, at least."

"It's the name for the people you call Crusading Hearts in your account."

She tucked a lock of hair under her headscarf and said:

"Anyway, the video of Amin killing Göran Loberg was the most viewed video in my time, in the Sweden I remember. It was like, always on…at bus stops and on the web…"

"And as you remember it, Amin killed Loberg?"

"Yes. And then his sister blew up the store. Just like our plan. But they didn't usually show that part when they used the video in PSAs and stuff. With the blood and the explosion. But if you searched for it online you could see it."

What did I think she could answer? Which question? She turned toward the window again. The blanket of clouds outside seemed to hover just above the ground, stifling and heavy. Worry flickered across her face and she said: "Maybe they made it up." Her finger began following the steel thread in the glass again. "Maybe they were just lying, I don't know."

On my cellphone's screen, the seconds and minutes tallied what was being recorded. She said, "You're wondering if I feel guilty about the people who got shot in the mosque, in the Rabbit Yard, yeah? By that racist. That's also why you're here, right?" She nodded in the direction of the doctor and added: "He gives me the news sometimes."

She was right, of course: deep down I did blame her for the intensifying hatred of Islam in recent years, but I realized that I didn't know who I, sitting there in that room with her, was to direct that accusation at her, so I kept quiet.

"I've written more," she said and handed me the papers.

"What do you want me to do with this?"

"Read it."

"And then? What do you want to happen to this…story?"

"It's your call."

I searched her eyes for something I could recognize—human contact, or guilt, after all, guilt over the world she'd helped create. There was nothing but a sucking dark absence.

"You gonna read it?"

"Now?"

"Yeah," she said, but I put the papers aside and leaned back, in part to make a point.

"So what was in those contracts you wrote about?"

"The citizen contract?"

"Yes," I said. "What was it that people refused to sign that landed them in the Rabbit Yard?"

She shrugged. "All sorts of stuff. Things about Islam and other religions. Hasn't a contract like that appeared in this world yet?"

I shook my head and she gave it some thought, seemed relieved, then said, "The contract had a whole bit about Sweden being special because it was the only country in the world where there was no racism. Mom used to laugh at that." She smiled, and then seemed to sink into herself. "There were pictures too. Göran Loberg's illustrations and other images, of Muslims and black people and stuff...illustrations from old children's books. And when you signed the contract you were, like, signing off on the value of all of those pictures, or... how should I put it? That you supported the illustrators."

I wanted to splash my face with cold water.

"Do you remember anything from when you were tortured? In al-Mima?"

"I'm telling you, that wasn't me." She looked down at her hands and I thought I saw her expression of horror or disgust. "I'm not from there."

I'm writing to you because you know how the violence feels.

I'm writing to you because you've also felt your body go tense with worry, limp and clumsy.

I looked up into the snow falling over the courtyard.

"What are you gonna do after high school?"

The bottle Liat had in her pocket was already half empty. She took another gulp and replied:

"I'm trying to get lit and you wanna know what's up after high school." She hadn't had that much to drink but was already slurring—either she was exaggerating or there was something else in the bottle too, yani dope.

My arms were hooked around the swing's chains, hands in my pockets, freezing.

"Just wondering."

The men must've taken the bus, because they came from the bus stop. As they marched our way, we jumped off the swings and made for my building because we could guess what they were, but they caught up with us and encircled us.

I don't remember what they looked like: when I think about them, their faces are just empty holes.

Their shoes creaked in the snow.

"Are you Muslims?" The guy talking sounded upset, he was breathing fast and seemed to be afraid of himself, of what he might do.

Before I could answer his question, Liat said, "Yes, *alhamdulillah* we are Muslims." She looked at him defiantly.

"We don't want Muslims here." I remember his cap pulled down over his forehead, the angular metal pin stuck in it, like a snowflake crossed with a swastika: the symbol of the Crusading Hearts. Another guy, a *shishko*, yani fatty, added:

"You and your fucking pedophile religion."

Shishko's hands were red and blotchy, and I remember those disgusting words: pedophile religion. I wanted someone else to be seeing what was happening, so I looked for someone in the buildings all around. A cigarette flashed on a balcony on the fifth or sixth floor but all of our windows were dark: Mom and Dad must have been in the living room or in their bedroom, both of which faced the willow tree.

"We're conducting a citizen's interrogation," one of the men said, and even though I don't remember his face I can tell you he looked like anyone, like any skinny old Swedish man who plays the lottery and is strict with children. "According to the February Laws, we have a right to interrogate suspected enemies of Sweden." He was pulling a small black dog on a leash so tightly he was almost strangling it.

The snow fell around us, slowly, like that white fluff inside pillows.

I remember thinking how we were inside a glass vacuum chamber.

"Well then I can interrogate you, too," Liat said, "because I'm also a citizen."

That made the shishko and another one of the guys laugh out loud, as if Liat's sass gave their game a new and unexpected, but welcome, dimension. But the guy with the cap grabbed hold of her jacket so hard the fur trim came loose—by the way, that was the jacket she would give me later, another winter.

"You aren't citizens," he hissed.

"And your breath smells like a fucking urinal," Liat said, tearing herself free and trying to push her way out of the crowd, but the men pressed together to stop her. She spun around and tried to push her way through in another spot. When that didn't work either, she went still.

She fingered the torn collar. I remember her hand shaking, and that this was the first time I'd seen her scared.

"You owe me four grand." That's what the jacket would've cost if it hadn't been a knockoff that she'd bought out of the trunk of a car. The men laughed again, and the old man with the dog demanded to see our passports. He typed our numbers into his phone and when he saw that we weren't on the list of enemies of Sweden he snorted and threw our passports in the snow. I remember their winter boots. Bluish snow. The gold lettering on the passport glimmering in the streetlight: *Sweden*.

Liat picked up the passports and tried to get out of the circle again, and the faceless men reluctantly let her through; I ran after her.

We went to my building. I tasted blood and was digging my nails into my frozen palms so hard it hurt, a dull pain. When the man with the dog shouted after us, a blast of sound like *aha* or *well, well* or *hello*, I took a few bounding steps, but the men just laughed again, triumphantly and mockingly, and I understood it was only a joke, he was just showing us who was boss.

I sat in my room and watched the snow bury the playground. The men had vanished. I wanted to write about how fear clogs the body like the hair in the school's shower drain, but I didn't have the words for Sensly. Maybe because I wasn't using my own face.

I clicked on the video again. He looked right at me. Amin. Like in my dreams. I thought he looked serious, weighed down by his destiny, but maybe bolstered by it too.

Interwoven, the two of us.

I clicked play on the video, the blade of the knife moved across that fucking artist's throat, the blood that spilled out was like black paint in the flashing blue lights coming in from the street.

I clicked on the video again, freezing it.

She sat at the kitchen table cutting up her credit cards. The grip she had on the scissors as she cut through the hard plastic made her look angry and crazy. I knew she was cutting up her cards because she'd refused to sign the citizen contract: the bank accounts of people who became enemies of the Swedish state were frozen at the same time as they lost their citizenship, so those cards would be useless soon. She swept the plastic slivers into her hand, threw them in the sink, and started on the next card.

When she saw me at the kitchen door she put the scissors down.

"We have the tickets. We're going to Algeria."

My legs almost gave out under me. I didn't like Sweden, and sometimes I longed for Algeria, but I couldn't leave Liat. Mom looked at me. I can't remember the color of her eyes.

"Don't be afraid," she said, because she mistook my

sadness for worry. "It's much easier to leave this country than it is to get in."

I don't remember if she and Dad fought about the contract again. I don't remember what Martin, Liat's new boyfriend, was like, or if I ever met him, or if Oh Nana Yurg had dropped another playlist.

There were a lot of demonstrations that spring, Swedes protesting the fact that some of the people who were fleeing large floods in Southeast Asia had made their way to Sweden. Liat and I saw the crowds through the bus and streetcar windows, waving flags in the rain, and sometimes counter-protesters were there too, small black-clad groups being led away by police.

Our family's plan was to travel to Algeria from Germany. Before she lost her Swedish citizenship, Mom had been a dual citizen, so she might not end up in the Rabbit Yard if she was arrested—she could also be deported. But here's the thing: just as likely as being allowed to go back to Algeria was ending up in one of the camps in Turkey or the Ukraine, where refugees arrested at the border were sent, so it was important we leave Sweden in secret.

We lived in a shadow world. We kept the blinds down all day and looked through the peephole for minutes at a time before leaving the apartment. A couple times guards from the housing authority rang our bell, and even though Dad talked to them through the door, without letting them in, my mother hid in the bathroom.

I remember the iWatch14 was released that year, and a sex tape featuring Oh Nana Yurg and a Japanese model called Tudi was leaked. For weeks I watched it several times a day, searching for something beautiful in those shaky images and in Oh Nana Yurg's eyes staring blindly into the dark. They were doing it on a hotel bed in Hong Kong and their bodies looked pale green, like lizard bellies. I wondered if that was the kind of thing Liat did with her boyfriend.

When I told her about Algeria, we were sitting in her room searching for news about Tudi on our smartphones, and she said wallah without looking up and I said wallah and saw her eyes go all shiny. I wanted to hug her and tell her I didn't want to go, but I didn't. Who knows if that was true anymore? Everything would be different in Algeria, and I'd started to long for it more and more since Mom had said the trip was actually happening. I thought wanting to go there was enough to mean I'd be welcome once I arrived, but I would've been wrong.

Dad and I visited the last mosque in Gothenburg. It was in an industrial building on Hisingen and the people who ran it had made compromises so they wouldn't lose their lease, like letting the Secret Service install camera globes at the entrance and replacing the usual Korans with new Swedish ones with blue-and-yellow covers and edits to the verses about war, the ban on charging interest, men and women, and stuff like that.

It was weird but that was where the contact who was going to help us get to Germany wanted to meet. Dad spoke in low voices with the man, off in a corner of the blue carpet, while I flipped through a blue-and-yellow Koran. As we were leaving, Dad nodded at me and said it was done, the arrangements for the trip had been made.

One day I asked Mom why Dad didn't keep any of the books he'd written at home. Incense was burning in the green dish, and she sat down next to me on the sofa.

"Do you remember what he was like when you were younger?" she asked.

"He wasn't always like this, huh?"

"What do you remember him being like?" Her voice was a rough, probing whisper, and I searched for a word that wouldn't betray Dad.

"Closer," I said. "He was closer to us, closer to the world."

She nodded, more to herself than to me. Her eyes reflected the willow tree and the apartment blocks, shrunk down so they all could have fit in a drop of water.

"That attack happened," she said. "The one where they went into the comic book store and killed people. ISIS was still called Daesh then. Your dad tried to write about it. But he couldn't."

"Why?" I thought I was on to something, something that could explain why I was dreaming of Amin, and why Dad hadn't told me about his books of poetry, but Mom threw open her hands in a gesture that meant only God knew.

"He told me he published his books in a different time. What did he mean?"

"I don't know, darling." She shook her head and was sort of absent, like she'd been sent back to that time, and said: "He wrote a book about it, in the end. But he was harshly criticized for it. Sweden had changed without him having noticed. After that he started hating his other books."

A stifling calm filled the living room, and I thought I saw a shadow around her. "He burned up every copy he could find of the books he'd written that the Swedes had liked."

In the images from the floods in Southeast Asia, rain clouds were rolling in from the ocean and towered over the horizon like mountain ranges, giant waves rolled in between crumbling skyscrapers and washed away traffic signs and roofs and people, and I thought how a storm was raging in Sweden too, a storm of emptiness moving through the trees.

"Yo."

"Lay off, I'm busy."

"Yo."

"Stop it."

"Yo."

"Come on, stop it, I'm watching the news."

Liat unwrapped a lollipop and tossed the wrapper aside, it spun away in the wind, a metallic strip glinting in the light. She bit off some of the lollipop and said, "Oh, so she's watching the news. The girl is serious."

They attacked Algeria four days before our flight was scheduled to leave Germany. The suicide bombers made their way into several mosques, and one group took hostages at a resort and blew themselves up when the military tried to get in. I remember Mom and Dad sitting with their packed bags, crying.

A nuclear bomb was detonated only a few days later. The news said that someone had put a Chinese nuclear warhead in a truck parked in central Algiers. Videos of blurry flames and whirling building dust floated together in my mind with images of the empty storm blowing through Sweden and Oh Nana Yurg's sex tape. All the same colorless shaky images.

"Yo."

"Not now."

"Yo."

"What?"

"Yo, I just want to ask you something."

"Wallah, ask."

"Yo."

I, like, never went to school that year, I couldn't cope, #no_future anyway, plus Mom was super depressed after Algeria and didn't have it in her to login and check my attendance anymore.

"Yo, just one question. It's important."

The second to last summer of freedom.

"What?"

"Yo."

The second to last breath.

"What?"

"Yo. What are you doing after high school?"

"Ha ha."

Liat was way hung over, she kept leaning forward in the swing like she needed to throw up, but didn't. She'd broken up with Martin and didn't have a boyfriend. Her dad had been in the Rabbit Yard for more than two years, her mom was unemployed, and she thought everything was useless, wallah.

"Yo, Liat?"

"Fuck that."

"Liat."

"Uh huh?"

"You know Amin?"

"The terrorist?"

I nodded and kicked the sand and felt everything I didn't have the words for spread inside me like a drop of black ink in water. "I dream about him. Like, we're riding on a moped or sitting around talking. Or I'm with him when he smokes that guy."

Liat laughed.

"Sick."

Our doorbell rang. I looked through the peephole. It was dark out there, and I thought the emptiness had finally swallowed everything, but obviously somebody was covering the hole, and I remembered a movie were a guy gets shot standing like that, peering out. I took a few steps back. The doorbell rang again.

Maybe it was Liat. The girl made jokes.

Mom was in the kitchen drinking tea and I sat down with her.

"They're covering the peephole," I said, but she barely seemed to hear me. She was twirling a couple of locks of her long black hair and staring at the kitchen cabinets. I said, "It's just some kids."

She'd started taking sleeping pills after what happened in Algeria and it weighed her down. When the doorbell rang again she looked up at me and smiled dozily.

"We're a love poem," she said. "Do you know that?" She made a gesture that took in our kitchen, the dirt on the windows, the swings outside, the bus stop. "You and me," she said, "and even the people out there ringing the doorbell. Everything is God's love poem to the Prophet."

We sat in silence. The buzz of the doorbell filled the apartment again and again, but after a while they gave up and slid a piece of paper through the mail slot, saying they suspected an enemy of the state was hiding with us and they were going to report it to the landlord. At the bottom of the page someone had drawn the symbol for the Crusading Hearts in pen. From the kitchen window, I looked across the yard and saw the man with the little black dog, the one who'd been with the guys who'd stopped me and Liat, walking past the swings.

Dreams about Amin, bright and self-contained, hard like pearls.

He kissed me between my shoulder blades. I said, "Amin?"

He replied, "Hamad."

A sharp crash woke me up. I lay there, staring at the ceiling, and when I couldn't fall back asleep I put on my sweatpants and went into the living room.

Mom and Dad stood in a sea of shattered glass. First I thought Mom was holding a shard too, but it was a kitchen knife—the big one with the triangular blade that she and Dad used to gut fish.

"Mom?" I remember her nightgown fluttering, and that's what made me realize somebody had broken the window. "What's on the floor?" I asked. Something big and dark was among the glass. Dad replied without turning around:

"It's just a stone. Don't turn on the light." A nauseating, sweet smell, like garbage filled the room.

"That's no stone," Mom kept repeating: "That's no stone." Her voice rose and became more piercing. "That's no stone."

I think each of us was going mad, each in our own way.

Dad slowly backed away from the window, and repeated:

"Don't turn on the light. If they're going to..." He didn't finish the sentence, to try to shield me from the knowledge of the threat that I nonetheless knew hung over us now. *If they're going to shoot. Kill us because we're Muslim.* I remember my parents' frozen silhouettes, and a cloud, backlit by the moon, floating through the glass on the floor. I remember the sound of cars passing by on the road beyond the willow tree and the field, and I felt like the apartment was floating in space, and that each second was stretching into an eternity. In the end I was the one who broke the stillness and turned on the light so we could see what was on the floor: a pig's head.

Amin. Elongated flashes of blue light reflected in his dark eyes. His pale lips. His sunken cheeks. I sat on my bed. I started the video and Amin sliced Loberg's throat, his body twitched and struggled, eyes wide open.

Maybe he was trying to scream behind that silver tape.

A mosaic of amber-colored shadows fell across the scratched linoleum floor in the visitor's room, over the plastic furniture, the desk, and the pine bookshelf and the walls that were scarred with misdirected rage. She was sitting in a chair and watching me closely as I read. Beads of sweat had formed on her forehead, along the edge of her headscarf. The air was hot and thick, as though we were waiting for a thunderstorm that would never come. I set the papers aside.

"How far have you gotten?"

"To...the pig's head."

"Do you like it?"

"No," I said. "But you can write," I added, which made her smile, lost and disarmed.

"I wrote lots on Sensly."

"You say here that you were Sufis?"

"It was mostly Mom who was into it," she said. "She used to get together with a group of sisters who did *dhikr* at our place in the evenings."

"But you people hate Sufism."

"Which 'people'?" she asked.

"Daesh," I said, and she looked away, rejected, possibly ashamed.

The word *dhikr* means "mentioning," but it's just as much about forgetting. For example, you repeat God's name or a mantra, in order to forget the dust of the world, in search of a trance state, a paradise state, prehistorical, pre-identity.

I crossed my legs, waited.

The professed Orthodox forms of Islam, which in part are kind of a shadowy mirror image of modernity, actively resist the practices that sometimes fall under Sufism, among them the many forms of dhikr: they're not allowed to enter mosques, those who practice are considered renegades, their books have been burned and graves considered sacred by some practitioners destroyed.

Without making eye contact she said:

"I mean. I didn't remember all of what I'm describing when I was with Amin and Hamad. I didn't remember who I was or where I came from. Otherwise I would've hated them."

The doctor stayed in his corner, observing the girl. I kept expecting him to chime in, like now when he moves his head a little or clears his throat, but he remained an observer, mute.

"What was it you saw in them? In Amin and Hamad?" I asked.

She replied, "I was drawn to them by a power that..." She still hadn't looked up from her hands, her finger was moving, scratching the top of her other hand. She never finished the explanation, instead she said, "I saw Amin on the streetcar one day, and I knew his name. I just knew, you know? *Your name is Amin.* And it was like I knew every line in his face. So I followed him into a building and we started talking in the elevator." Some large emotion quivered behind those downcast eyes. "That's how we met."

She stopped speaking. Twilight fell, a silvery cornflower blue and a welcome coolness. I listened to the building's dull, indistinct sounds—water streaming through the pipes, noise from fans, footsteps somewhere overhead.

I'd read versions of her encounter with Amin in various articles. They got to know each other quite soon after she'd arrived in Gothenburg, and began a relationship.

It was like I knew every line in his face. Falling in love probably always contains an element of madness. It was like that for me and Isra many years before, when we met at the university where she then worked.

"The Prophet," she said after a while, finally making eye contact, inviting me in with that secretive, half-pleading way of hers.

"*Salla llahu 'alay-hi wa-sallam*," I said—may God's blessings and peace be with him.

"He found a crying man," she said. "The sun had set before the man had a chance to pray his afternoon prayer." This was a *hadith*, one of the tens of thousands of accounts of the Prophet's life and deeds collected in books and oral traditions. I happened to know the story, which is about God's power over time, and I continued for her:

"The Prophet prayed to God, asking him to allow the man to say his prayers in time."

"Salla llahu 'alay-hi wa-sallam," she said.

"Salla llahu 'alay-hi wa-sallam. And the sun rose again over the horizon," I said. I believe, as many Muslims do, that this actually happened, it's a historical fact: two men crouching in the desert, the sun rising in the west and making their shadows pull back in, backward into their bodies. Backward into history.

"I mean, I'm not saying it was God," she said.

"Who sent you back in time?"

She glanced out the window. In the deep stillness of the room, the movement seemed rushed and sweeping.

The time for evening prayer had come. Maybe that's what she was thinking about.

"Sometimes I dream about things that must've happened in her childhood," she said. "The Belgian girl, the one they say I am."

"What do you dream?"

"Short scenes. A man tosses me up in the air and catches me. I walk on a beach, my toes dig into the sand."

"So now you know that you're her? Annika?"

She shrugged, then said, "I know this body once went by that name, and used to live in Belgium, and later was tortured. But I also know that I'm not her. I'm someone else, someone who came here from the future. That Annika might've died if I hadn't woken up in her body. Maybe she died in my world, instead of Amin's sister, or something."

I *hmmed* in reply. She'd given this a lot of thought.

I'd been having trouble sleeping. The tiredness rose behind my eyes like sharp flickering static. Something else was bothering me, a worry at work inside me that I had to address while I was there.

"You don't remember a…time machine?" I asked, and had to laugh at the word, but when I listened to the recording later, I realized that's right when I moved the conversation away from reality: shifting focus away from the fact that she, in spite of everything, was a girl from Belgium, and back to her misconceptions.

It was because of what was unclear inside me. What I hadn't managed to examine, what frightened me and made me want to keep coming back.

For a long time I thought it was all about the writing.

"I ended up somewhere, in the end," she replied. "But it's hard to organize the events in my head. That's also why I'm writing them down." Her eyes rested on the stack of paper in my hands and then I sensed a more familiar worry in her: even if we were discussing a fantasy, she'd still revealed something personal.

"Why did you come back?" she asked. In the silence that followed I once again became aware of the din of rushing water and clattering fans. A voice came through the floor or the wall—a scream cut short. The waiting room quality of the place. Hades. My eyes focused on a mark on the wall where someone must have slammed a piece of furniture. The mark could also have been made by a skull or elbow.

"I came back because of what happened at Hondo's," I said. "Because of what you did that night."

Her gaze darkened and drifted out the window into the night outside.

She turns the flashlight on her smartphone off.

"What, did the battery die?" Amin lets the blade drop, exhausted, as though he had been powered by the light and can no longer hold up the small box cutter.

He's still got a hold on Loberg's hair, trying to maintain a decent grip, and she watches him claw at the sweaty white mop, thinking: Amin is clinging to the edge of an abyss.

Out in the winter night the police shout into a megaphone. The amplified voice is hard to understand. Something about talking. *Talk to us.*

She notices Amin squinting, straining to see her in the dark store.

"Your nose is bleeding again," he says. "Why aren't you filming?"

Impossible to answer. Can hardly think about it. The future. She comes from the fucking future.

Loberg's feet are sliding around in the blood. Mumbled groans come from behind the duct tape.

"Nour?" Amin says, the name he uses that doesn't belong to her, but to his sister, the girl who died in a bathtub in this world, but who was with them in her world, instead of her.

"I remember you." She lifts up her phone. "From here. From this video."

"What are you talking about?"

She's speaking to Amin, who used to tell her she was his dead sister returned—she says:

"I'm not from here."

"From Gothenburg?"

She's only saying it now.

"I am not from this time." She gets a blinding headache, it makes it hard to think. She runs her sweater sleeve along her upper lip but can tell all she's doing is smearing the nosebleed across her face.

She'd like to crumple to the floor and cry for everything. For Liat and Mom and Dad.

"We're going to wake up all of Europe's Muslims," Amin says—those are just Hamad's words, they don't mean anything anymore.

They're facing each other, hunched in the blue light as the din from the street clamors in the venue. Around them, the hostages in their black hoods are bowed over. She thinks they look like those hangmen back when there were crusaders—like those ripped guys with mega axes.

"Amin. I don't know how, but I've come here from the future."

She thinks the room is turning itself inside out, the corners pushing inward, and she stumbles backward, trying not to fall.

She remembers. She closes her eyes and sees a clap of pigeons rising past the flickering LCD screen down at the bus stop. Past Amin's face. She's on the verge of falling backward again, and a sharp blade slides between her eyes. She remembers everything. The footbridge. The room with the aluminum boxes. The pair of empty swings rocking in the wind.

I'm writing to what's inside you that we've lost in ourselves. Writing to your eyes, to your eyelashes, your lips and cheeks, to your tongue.

Mom and I climbed over the steep slabs of rock at the beach and threw ourselves shrieking into the waves, their snowy green explosions. We liked swimming in late fall, when we could be alone. We swam a few strokes out into the chilly water, teeth chattering, then turned back and crawled, blue and cold, up over rocks slick with algae.

We sat wrapped in our towels, and Mom, who was finally starting to get over her depression, looked out over the sea and said:

"There are trees out there, beneath the surface."

"Trees?"

"Everything there is on land has a counterpart in the sea. There are mountains in the sea. Storms that rage under the ocean's surface."

That was Sufism, yani mysticism.

A seagull dove overhead at the same time as it seemed to be rising from the dark pitching waves, the image fluttered like a white sheet. It is said that our actions echo in the sky, but maybe the sea is that sky.

"There are seahorses," I shivered, half serious, half joking. "Sea cucumbers." That last one made Mom laugh.

When it was time for afternoon prayer we used our towels as prayer mats, and when we bowed down it was like God was impressed on the rough surface of the rocks and in the roar of the wind and sea. While we were still kneeling, she turned to me. She took her headscarf off and her hair blew around her face, and right then I thought she looked as ancient as the rock we were on, and it was like I didn't know her at all.

"Whatever happens, I want you to remember one thing," she said. Rain clouds had gathered in dark blue and black layers behind her, and between us was something that had to do with God, but also with two people at this point in history, two Muslims in Sweden, seventeen years after the attack on Hondo's, and she reached out and touched my cheek and the wind picked up and her smile frightened me. "Remember," she said. "We are a love poem."

She went missing later that night. She used to go for walks when it stormed so she could be alone on the streets, and when she'd been gone for two hours and hadn't answered her phone Dad put on his red raincoat and crossed the fields past the willow tree, and I went in the other direction, toward the square and the bus stop. After a while I couldn't stop shouting:

"Mom! Mom!" My voice felt weak and small, swallowed by the night like something sinking into mud, gone.

When I approached the footbridge where Liat and I would sometimes stand and spit I saw the yellow lights of a patrol car flaming in the rain and had an awful premonition.

I ran onto the bridge.

She was on her back across the hood of a car down there, her head sunk through the crushed windshield. Somebody had pushed her. I looked into her open mouth. The raindrops falling between her lips seemed to darken and disappear.

I stumbled through the bushes, onto the road, and the lights seeping into the wet asphalt made me think of what she'd said by the sea, about, like, mirror worlds, and time seemed to be going backward, or at least in some different direction, sideways.

The car she'd landed on after she was thrown over the railing must have skidded, because it was parked crooked in the middle of the road. A couple of other cars had stopped along the curb and the rain hung like tinsel in their headlights.

Everything was wrong.

Someone kept honking—angry, drawn-out sounds that cut through the wind and rain.

Balagan.

Balagan.

In addition to the patrol car blocking the traffic was an ambulance, but instead of helping Mom the EMTs were flipping through what I could tell was her passport—checking it against a smartphone. I think her insurance was invalid because she was an enemy of Sweden, and they were trying to figure out who was going to pay for her care. The reflective strips on their clothing gleamed.

I crawled onto the hood of the car. I remember praying to God as I slipped around on that wet metal sheet. *Change it. Do everything different.* A guard spotted me and ran over.

"She's alive," I said. "She's still alive." I lifted her head up. It was like a bundle of wet fabric, and I remember that the guard issued an order and his voice was firm, but the words didn't reach me.

"Mom," I said. She registered my presence, her lips moved, and she said:

"There is no God." Her eyes were like fogged glass, water ran from her clothing and hair, out over the hood of the car, in pink streams, and she said:

"There is no God but God."

The guard pulled me away, and the leaves whipping across the road looked like curls of ash rising from a fire.

In Hondo's window display was a row of French comics in plastic sleeves. The various covers were a mash-up of a polished-chrome, kitschy futuristic aesthetic and a Stone Age world, all of it vaguely pornographic and priced around the thousand kronor mark.

I stuffed my kufi in my shoulder bag before walking through the door.

Right before closing time, not many customers. I was hoping to chat with the owner, Christian Hondo, who had been there the night of February seventeenth. I didn't see him.

I'd passed by the store countless times but had never been inside. The space was smaller than I'd imagined after seeing it in the photos, hardly bigger than a living room. I flipped through a comic book—an issue of *X-Men* I'd read as a child—and looked around.

I saw the corner where the girl had filmed Amin with her smartphone.

That's where the black flag had hung.

The stage.

The feeling that I might be exposed, discovered with my thoughts.

I went over to the spot, dragged my shoe across the floor, wondering if it had been replaced or if Göran Loberg's blood had merely been scrubbed away.

"We're closing soon," said a woman behind the counter. Even though it was a hot September day, she was dressed in black layers. Her dress had buckles and leather straps over the chest and arms.

I looked up at the ceiling and found a small bullet hole near the exit, where Amin had fired his gun.

I wanted to experience something that would give me clarity and make me hate the girl from Tundra.

I took the comics I'd been flipping through to the checkout, mostly to have an excuse to talk to the salesperson.

"So Christian isn't working today?"

She punched in the price, which I hadn't even checked. It was much more than I would've guessed.

"He doesn't work here anymore," she replied.

"Did he sell the store?"

She gave me a practiced dismissive look. People must come in here asking for Christian Hondo a couple times each week, for reasons that all had to do with the events of February seventeenth, and I suspected that she was debating whether or not to ask me to leave.

"I'm writing a book about what happened here," I added. "I'm an author."

"And you want to talk to Christian?"

"If possible..."

She was still holding the comic book. "And this?" she said. "Did you actually want to buy it?"

Christian Hondo lived one block from the store, which he still owned. The woman closed the store, locked up, and called him from a Thai restaurant on the corner—apparently a daily delivery of takeout at the end of business hours was now part of the job description.

I flipped absentmindedly through my far-too-expensive childhood souvenir as they spoke. Hondo must have asked my name, because the woman had me repeat it and then said it into her cellphone. She waited—my guess is that Hondo was googling me.

She bought two Thai dishes and explained, without me having asked, that Hondo saved one of them for lunch the next day. I made sure she didn't see my kufi as I stuffed the comic book in my shoulder bag.

Hondo's apartment was cluttered with posters, books, stray papers, sculptures, trash.

We sat in the kitchen. The woman from the store had dropped off the food and left.

"I rarely get out nowadays," Hondo said, eating straight out of the box with the splintery wooden chopsticks that came with the food—a noodle dish with bean sprouts and egg. In an overly formal tone and with a touch of self-deprecation, he added, "Feeding the owner is now part of the employment contract."

Out the window, between the office buildings and rental apartments of City West, the Denmark ferry passed by, gliding slowly into harbor.

"Is this because of what happened on February seventeenth?"

Hondo wound the noodles around the chopsticks and slurped them down. My question might have been too forward. He seemed to be deciding whether to lie or ask me to leave.

"You could say," he said, "I'm suffering from a certain... ochlophobia." He whipped the chopsticks around in the air. "Fear of crowds." His laugh was affected. "A phobia of visiting places where terrorists might strike."

His face was ruddy, he had a pronounced overbite, and he was dressed in a T-shirt and jeans. I'd put him at around forty years old. He had a tic that made his mouth jump, and something made me think he talked to himself, held long monologues in the empty apartment.

"Do you feel hatred?"

"Hatred?"

"Antipathy? Vengefulness?"

He left the living room, fetched a large art book, and put it down in front of me. Drawings with a 1970s aesthetic, all politically provocative and with a sexual undertone. Genitals in the colors of the Swedish flag, the royal family in their underwear.

"I exhibited these in the '90s." He tucked a strand of long hair behind his ear to keep it from falling in the food. "Pretty banal, one might say." I rocked my head in an ambiguous nod. "They tried to burn the store down," he said. "Back then it was skinheads." He slurped up another mouthful of noodles. "I don't hate people. I want to rattle their preconceptions of the world. Their assumptions about morals, about nations. About themselves. Have you read de Sade?"

"A long time ago. At university." He gestured with his chopsticks again, inviting me to fill in the rest myself.

"They wanted to murder me," he said. "All I want is to murder God."

When he'd finished eating he fetched medicine from a kitchen cabinet, shook out three small yellow pills, and washed them down with a few gulps of soda. I read what it said on the bottle, which he'd left in view, something for anxiety.

He didn't ask me about the book I'd said I was writing, what it would be about, or who else I'd met with. I didn't stay long. I asked a lot about the attack, about what he remembered, but mostly because I thought it was expected of me. He didn't follow me to the door on my way out. Instead he waited nervously in the living room as I tied my shoes in the hall. It occurred to me that the woman who worked in the store had her own set of keys. She'd unlocked the front door and let herself in.

I remember him peering through the crack after I closed the door behind me.

"How's it going with your family?"

"Alhamdulillah," Mido said. We walked down Vasagatan Avenue, under the yellowing crowns of the trees. We had just left a screening of Mido's latest film, a documentary about the refugee crisis in the Mediterranean.

He was an old friend, a political activist more than a filmmaker, originally from Egypt.

"How's it going with you?"

"Alhamdulillah," I echoed. It was late afternoon, lots of people on the go, bicycles, strollers, briefcases. Mido's film had roused something in me. The pictures of rickety boats landing on slippery black rocks. A fiery field of empty life vests rocking in the swells. People fleeing their homelands. It was the day after my strange visit with Christian Hondo.

"Even though there's reason to worry, you know?" I said.

"About what?"

"About how the world is." I hadn't mentioned my visits to Tundra to anyone but Isra, and I didn't know how I would even begin to discuss the girl, her writing, the book I was maybe thinking about writing. “About what it will be like in Sweden in five years.”

Mido popped the collar of his blazer. He was a little older than me and his black shoulder-length hair was graying.

“We have to fight, brother,” he said. “We have to tell the Swedes our stories.”

“Yes,” I replied awkwardly. I’d always admired Mido’s pathos and frankness, which had once forced him to flee Egypt—he’d made films criticizing the regime that governed the country before the Arab Spring had turned into fall and now perhaps into an Arab Winter.

“Do you ever look at your children…” I said, but my voice caught. I was surprised how hard it was to express myself.

Mido’s eyes were charcoal-rimmed, black lines accentuating his almost bluish whites. He looked at me with curiosity.

“Do you ever look at them and wonder if they’re going to be able to live their lives here?” I said.

“Because they’re Muslim?”

“Because people are scared, and because in the end they’ll do anything to not feel that way.”

The trees behind Mido—all of those thousands of bright, yellowing leaves looked like the stained glass windows of a church.

I'm writing to those of you who still have words for what's happening to you and whose entire world is wrapped up in mine.

Your words, hemmed in by all I cannot say.

I stuffed half a potato in my mouth. "A girl in my class has a brother who's one of those, you know." I chewed for a long time before swallowing. "A Crusading Heart."

Dad put down his knife and fork, propped his elbows on the table, and pressed his fingers to his head as if he needed to keep it from exploding. I poked at my food, waiting for him to say something. I wanted him to ask for the name and address of the girl in my class so he could take his revenge on her brother.

The security company that handled traffic safety in our neighborhood had determined that Mom's death was a suicide, so the police didn't do anything. But I know someone pushed her. One of them. A Crusading Heart. Maybe the man with the black dog, whom I'd never seen again.

"She's a martyr," Dad said, his tone muted and strange. "Martyr." The word was the sound of a door slamming shut inside him.

The walls were covered in scuffed aluminum pigeonholes. One of the caretakers in blue overalls had let us in, and when Dad showed him our numerical code the man took out a big bunch of keys, riffled through them for a while, and then turned a lock, pulled out a box, and put it on the table.

Dad opened the box, his hands unsteady. I remember it clattering and thinking about how his hands had shaken when he read the poem about sharia to the Swedes.

What was in the box looked like volcanic sand or ground black chalk, and for a long time we just stared at it.

The caretaker jangled his keys impatiently.

Dad shoved his hand into the box and filtered the dusty matter between his fingers. Because Mom was an enemy of Sweden, she couldn't be buried in the country, so they'd cremated her, like automatically, even though she was Muslim.

We backed away and stood in a corner of the room, as the caretaker put the box back in the wall.

I remember Dad's hands, blackish gray with ash, and him not knowing what to do with them when we left that place: brush them off on his blazer or stuff them in his pockets or kiss them.

That was the winter Liat gave me her jacket because Dad had stopped working and we couldn't afford to replace my raggedy-ass old one.

You could say I was the one who ended up taking care of us. Cleaning and making food and stuff, frozen pizza and chips. If I had to make a list of all the lame things that happened after Mom's death, those goopy pizzas we used to eat would be number four; number three would be Dad not praying anymore. Number two would be that he got sloppy about taking his insulin, and his eyesight got so bad he sometimes couldn't see me and would shout my name loudly even though we were in the same room. Wallah, it made me feel like a ghost.

One night I was walking home from the bus stop with Liat. We'd been at the mall. I stopped and laid down on the asphalt. She stared at me and said, "Yo." She said, "Yo, what are you doing?" But I didn't reply. I just laid there and let the chill from the earth creep through my jacket into my life, and then she did the same thing, and took my hand, and we laid like that for a long time, silent next to each other, watching the perforated dome of darkness as stars spun away above us, and the tears in my eyes froze into snow.

Bummer number one: Dad would sit awake at night, hunched over his computer, writing. No news site would publish his article, so in the end he put it out on the web himself, and I read it and realized he was losing it. He wrote about us being annihilated because of a crack that was running right through Sweden. He wrote that language had once been a gift from God, but was now the devil's tool.

He had too many words in him and all of them were wrong.

He didn't sign the citizen contract that spring, and because he was now an enemy of Sweden and they were going to track him down to put him in the Rabbit Yard, we left our apartment and moved in with a couple he knew, a couple that had been there on that spring night he'd read his poem.

It was the year the iWatch 15 was released.

He told me to make sure no one was following me as I walked home from school.

Sometimes when I just couldn't deal, I slept at Liat's.

Time was God's fire, annihilating everything.

Along the bike paths, men in reflective vests used leaf blowers to make last year's dead leaves spin away in small cyclones.

The school guidance counselor clasped his hands on the table in front of him.

"Is your dad forcing you to do things?"

"Like, what things?"

"I've noticed you often wear a beanie sort of like a hijab, for instance. Pulled down over your hair." His bottom lip was pierced and his shirtsleeves were rolled up, exposing tattoos on his forearms. Horned Japanese demons with round, staring eyes. "Did you pick it out yourself?"

"I am Muslim, in case you didn't get that."

I'd automatically become an enemy of Sweden along with Dad, actually, but the law said even the children of enemies of Sweden had to stay in school, yani, partake in Swedish culture, and law enforcement wasn't allowed to take kids from school and put us in camps, so I was, like, safe there.

"Where do you live now?" the counselor asked, like I was actually going to tell him, right? So he could note it down in the same file the security companies had access to? I snapped my gum to show him what a dumb-ass he was. "Are you allowed to have a boyfriend?" he asked. "Why are you laughing?"

"I'm thinking about what I'm going to tell my friend about you."

Liat leaned back in her swing. She'd dyed her bangs the same light blue as Oh Nana Yurg's in the videos for her new acoustic playlist.

"How sweet is it that we never ever have to see that school again. It's like, 'Later, victims.'" The blue tufts of hair flickered like a lighter's flame. Amin's video was playing on the screen at the bus shelter; he looked at me as that line of text popped up.

It all could have been different.

I shut my eyes. Mom by the sea. Reaching out and touching me. When I opened my eyes, there was something finite about the dust in the air, something important had ended.

"What about us?" I said.

"What about us?"

"Will we always know each other?"

Liat stretched her legs up into the air and checked her sneakers for stains, a pair of Balenciaga knockoffs in pale leather that she was still trying to keep clean, even though one of the soles was already coming loose.

Over by the bus stop Amin put the knife to Göran Loberg's throat and the screen went black.

"Always," she said.

I'm not sure how long we lived with Dad's friends, it could have been a couple of weeks or six months, but it got messy with them in the end: they showed us an email from the landlord saying they'd be kicked out if we stayed there.

I remember that we were sitting at the kitchen table, their eyes pleading with us to leave, go out into the emptiness, so that they could get on with their lives.

We didn't sleep that night. Our mattresses were in their living room and Dad sat by the open balcony door, talking. I have a hard time remembering exactly what he said. Distance. Distance had spread between everything, he said. An attempt to put words to the emptiness, like when he wrote that nasty article. I pulled the blanket up to my chin and thought that maybe he was talking to the people who'd liked his books once upon a time, or with Mom. He said the devil was distance. Distance from God. Something like that. It was his grief talking. The tower he'd built. I remember being scared by his voice and his confused hand gestures, and that he'd stop talking mid-sentence.

Somewhere out in the courtyard a dog was barking.

"They reported themselves to the landlord," he said. "You understand that, right?"

We ended up at the mosque with the blue and yellow Korans, where Dad had once found the man who was supposed to smuggle us into Germany. Apparently, there was a back door with no cameras, and a secret room on the top floor. We lived with ten other families, crammed in with our bedding and bags.

Dad often read the Koran with the other men—not the blue and yellow ones stacked in the prayer room, but the real one, which people had brought with them.

I slept half the day away now that I wasn't in school anymore. At night I snuck out through the back door and went to a newsstand and bought an energy drink. We'd kept our cellphones off since Dad had become an enemy of Sweden, but there was a cellphone in the mosque I could borrow, and I called Liat during my walks.

"When are you coming back?" she asked, and I said I didn't know, but soon, *inshallah*. "Have you heard what they're saying about Oh Nana?"

"We, like, don't have internet here," I said, even though, real talk, since Mom died I couldn't have cared less about the latest on Oh Nana Yurg.

"They're saying she doesn't exist," Liat said. "She's just a computer program."

"Balagan."

"It's all over the web. They're saying a company created her and the songs were all written by a computer program." I noticed that Liat was trying to pretend she didn't believe it, but she was actually shocked. "I mean, they're saying it was just a hologram performing at her concerts."

I didn't know how to feel. I wasn't disappointed. Not even surprised. I was nothing, maybe. Liat kept talking, changed the subject eventually, and told me about who from our class had been in fights and who was going out with whom, but it was like she was talking about things happening in a country far, far away.

I bought my energy drink at the newsstand, and even though it was dangerous for me to be outside I stayed out. Steam rose from the vents of the laundry rooms in the buildings all around. I thought about Oh Nana Yurg, whom I'd loved so much.

Those of us hiding in the mosque who hadn't been to the Rabbit Yard yet were less afraid of going than the people who'd already spent time there. A woman around Mom's age who comforted me when I cried in my sleep said that the Rabbit Yard was a place where there was no truth, and I pictured a giant, rotating hole behind the fences and buildings, an emptiness surrounded by whirling leaves, bricks, road signs, and people. A lie.

A group of guys cooked soup for us. They served it out of the trunk of their minivan—steaming lentil soup ladled into paper bowls each night, five brothers with beards like old men.

Liat talked about guys and how rotten the Suedis in the class were being to her, and how she wished for school to end, and when I didn't respond we listened to each other breathing and then said goodbye.

Cities of frost appeared on the secret room's poorly insulated window.

One morning I heard voices from the ground floor—screaming in Arabic and Swedish: "Help, this is a democracy, we have rights, we are Swedish citizens." And the woman who comforted me when I cried ran into the room and hurled herself out the window, pulling the curtains and blinds behind her, like a broken wing of fabric and rustling aluminum strips.

We were led out to the parking lot, where ambulances and cars from various security companies were parked. Dad was wearing the tunic he usually slept in—it caught around his legs and made him trip when one of the guards prodded him on. His eyes met mine as he climbed into a white van.

Total balagan all around me, noise and screaming. The woman who'd jumped through the window was strapped to a cot carried by two orderlies. She pulled at the straps, making the cot rattle and seem ready to fall to pieces, but she didn't scream. Her leg was hurt: a shaft of bone stuck out from her skin like a broken, red-streaked halogen light.

I ended up in a van with four guys who were refugees from the floods, shy young people from, like, Nepal—they weren't Muslim but I remember them from the secret room, where they kept to themselves, quiet and polite.

When the van stopped a half-hour later and the doors opened, we were in a large garage; we were told to sit down on the cement floor. I hugged my knees and rubbed my arms to stay warm. I'd at least managed to bring my jacket and shoes, unlike lots of people, who were only in their T-shirts and socks.

The van left, more people arrived, and then even more people were brought out into that echoing, subterranean space, uneasy and cold. A group of guards in blue uniforms stood by an elevator door, conversing in low voices; they kept laughing at something, and after a while I got that they were talking about the girls, our looks or whatever.

About half of the people who'd been rounded up that morning had come from the mosque, the rest had probably been picked up in other hiding places, or had been arrested in raids on buses and streetcars. Most were Muslim, but there were also refugees from the floods and people who I think were Jewish or just regular Swedes—yani political extremists—and a group of beggars from southern Europe. I looked for Dad but didn't see him. Guards kept coming in and shouting names before taking people into the elevator, and after a few hours it was my turn.

The guard who led me through the garage, gently clasping my upper arm, was black-haired and could've had an African parent, and I thought he was betraying something I couldn't express.

The Swedes had decided he was Swedish.

I don't know how I ended up reuniting with Dad, but suddenly I was in a room where a woman who looked tired and overworked was shining a small lamp in his mouth. He was naked. His clothes were in a pile on the floor. I remember a pinewood desk and a bed with white plastic sheets. The woman wearing blue latex gloves was sticking a finger in Dad's mouth, pushing down his jaw.

A man in a knit sweater was standing by the desk, taking notes on a tablet. When he asked for my passport number, Dad turned around. He saw me and covered his genitals. The emptiness pressed against my temples. The woman told Dad to turn around and bend over. I can still hear the grim, wet sound of the soles of his feet on the floor as he moved. I remember the glossy surfaces in the room. As though it had been designed to be hosed clean. The woman took out a stethoscope and listened to Dad's lungs, and I wish I hadn't, but I saw his face. It was like any other body part now, an elbow or a patch of skin on his belly or thigh.

His eyes were fixed on the wall, motionless, as if his pupils were pinned in place with long needles.

The string was stretched between her fingers, like a web. She pinched it in two places then pulled them out, making the pattern even more complex.

A game to kill time while she waited for me to finish reading.

The doctor had written with a request for me to return. Apparently she had opened up after meeting me, and it had been established that our interactions were beneficial for her recovery.

Before reading even half, I put the papers down, and she seemed overcome by insecurity. She played down the anxiety with a kind of jokey hesitance—bit the string and used her teeth to pull out a loop that she then stuck her index finger through. She stretched it into an eight-pointed star, through which she looked at me.

A light rain whispered against the armored glass, the walls of the clinic, the roofing tiles.

"This inspection you're writing about," I said. "When they undressed your dad. What do you think that was about?"

She kept looking at me through the star, and instead of answering my question she said:

"Maybe I've been sent here on a mission, to your time, have you thought about that?"

I needed to stretch my legs, so I got up and stood by the window. The Bear Man was outside smoking, sheltered by an overhang.

"Do you remember anything like that?" I said. "Someone giving you a mission?"

"No."

"But you think that's what happened?"

"I mean, I know some things. One: I've traveled back in time. Yani, my soul traveled back in time and ended up in this body."

"In Annika Isagel's body."

"Exactly. Two: I ended up, like, out of whack, in a world where Amin's sister died, and where I almost took her place."

"And why do you suppose you've come here? What's your mission?"

"To stop Amin and Hamad of course, so the Swedes don't start killing us. Don't you think?"

When I failed to respond she broke eye contact. She busied herself with the string, stretching it into a new constellation, holding it out to me:

"Want to play? It's actually a game for two people."

I sat across from her and followed her instructions, pinched where she told me to, pulled the string out, wound finger after finger into what was taking shape between us.

"Liat taught me this, right after we met," she said, and showed me another shape. I accidentally touched her fingers.

I felt a swell of tenderness, unbidden but overwhelming. I could've cried, but swallowed hard. For a few seconds the intensity of the whispering rain increased, and then subsided.

She studied my face, curious. When I didn't say anything, she said:

"So...that inspection. I think it had something to do with the emptiness." Sometimes when she talked she mumbled like a child who's afraid of being punished. "It was inside of language, and made some things the same when they should have been different. Yani a Muslim equaled a terrorist. Or a nurse equaled a guard. There was no difference between the blood in my veins and Amin's knife. There was no difference between my heart beating and the bombs exploding in Algeria."

My daughter threw a snowball straight up into the creaking, infinite stillness of the sky. She was waddling around in her nylon jumpsuit, her mouth steaming among the gravestones, and I came to the sad realization that the child she was on that cold, quiet winter day, visiting my mom's grave...that child would disappear, or was already gone, destroyed by time.

I crouched down by the black stones. I prayed Mom knew the peace I did not. I looked out over the crystallized landscape, at the sparkling power lines and trees.

"Why did you come here?" I whispered into the crusty snow.

She hadn't told me much about the journey here, or about her family in Gambia. I knew she had crossed the Mediterranean illegally, and when we were in the mosque praying the funeral prayers for the relatives of congregation members who had died during similar trips, she'd always cried after, a helpless sobbing.

Eventually she'd been granted a residency permit and became Swedish, but she was afraid of the authorities here, afraid of the bank, afraid of the neighbors, and I'd always interpreted that as a remnant of her homeland, a shadow she'd brought with her across the sea, but now I wondered if it wasn't the other way around, if the fear didn't belong here, to this country.

"Why did you come to Sweden?" I touched the stone.

In Islam we believe that a grave is a door to an unknown kingdom, a barrier between this life and the next. A dark parallel of the uterus. We believe the dead are waiting to be born for a second time, from the earth, to face final judgment, and that their existence in the grave is a result of their actions in life. I asked God to watch over Mom and ease her trials out there, in the unknown.

According to a hadith, clay from this very grave plot was used when her body was created, in a Gambian woman's uterus almost a hundred years ago. It was already decided then that she would die in Sweden and be buried here, in this deep-frozen earth. The matter was always going to find its way back here. I looked up into the light. *What is it, then? Time. I don't know. A landscape.*

I found pictures of the girl from Tundra as a child, pictures from school and from social events. A regular Belgian girl. She had braces for a few years in middle school. Her parents were university graduates, well established. Whether or not she had sympathized with Daesh before she was abducted and taken to al-Mima was disputed. I tried to reach her parents. Her mother was still living in Brussels. I called and emailed her several times, but to no avail. There was no trace of her father after the attack on Hondo's—he'd simply moved without giving a new address. It was no surprise that the family was hard to get ahold of—they'd been stalked by the media and harassed by racists.

I wrote to Amin's mother and Hamad's parents. Unlike Amin's father, who lived in Norway, they still lived in Gothenburg. No reply.

Göran Loberg was in a secret location and had a twenty-four-hour security detail, but I wrote to an email address I found on his blog, and to the publisher of his book of caricatures.

I still didn't know if I would write the book, but I sensed that I had to find out something about the girl, find out why I was the one she'd contacted, and what had actually happened at Hondo's that night.

I told Mido about my visits to the asylum. He was surprised, intrigued, and asked if he could bring his camera, but I didn't think it was a good idea. I wanted to preserve what had arisen between me and the girl, whatever it was.

I read everything I could find about al-Mima. It wasn't actually a proper prison, but a camp erected in the desert outside Amman in the years after September 11. I saw the pictures. The guard towers monitoring modular buildings made of concrete and plywood. Military tents flapping in the wind. Rows and rows of cages lined up in the heat. A landscape beyond the law.

Mostly suspected terrorists and so-called "unlawful combatants" from countries in the Third World ended up in al-Mima, but several European and American citizens had been sent there to be subjected to interrogation methods that were legally and politically impossible in their home countries. In addition to the girl from Tundra, it is said that a Swedish citizen with Somali heritage was there for a time. His name was only mentioned on the record once in Sweden: he was cited as a source in an article in *Aftonbladet*. I emailed the journalist, requesting to be put in touch with him, but the reply took its time.

Al-Mima had been shut down and razed to the ground when a bunch of documents and films from inside had leaked to the media.

Mainly the leaked material showed how prisoners were subjected to the interrogation methods recognizable from other so-called "black sites": waterboarding, sexual and religious humiliation, dogs, electricity, long-term isolation, forced feeding. Among these better known images another set of material was unnoticed, one that seemed to bear witness to more bizarre and inexplicable treatment. There were photographs showing people on a cement floor with wires operated into their bodies or stuck into suction cups all over their skin. In some pictures they seemed to be being subjected to brain surgery without anesthesia.

Eyewitness testimonies from al-Mima often had internal contradictions and were otherwise confused: the victims spoke of having been injected full of chemicals and connected to computers, being submerged in saltwater tanks, sensory deprivation. At least three victims described their experiences in al-Mima in religious terms, saying their souls had been taken out of their bodies or that they had been possessed by djinns—invisible beings that, according to Islam's expansive and multidimensional cosmology, were created by desert winds and fire before the time of man.

The prison hadn't been manned by standard guards or military personnel but by employees of K5GS, and the suspicions about the company, among which were reports from Amnesty International and Human Rights Watch, suggested the company had used the prisoners in al-Mima as guinea pigs in neurological experiments.

After the prison closed down, the majority of the

prisoners were lost to other types of confinement, and the few who once again saw the light of day were hardly in a state to give a clear account of what they'd endured.

It was there, in the Jordanian desert, at the border of technology and theology, that the girl in the clinic had been put into the unreachable, peculiar state she had been found in following her repatriation to Belgium.

I was at my living room window. Isra was playing with our daughter down in the courtyard—the girl fell into a snow drift, ice and snow got inside the fur collar of her snowsuit and Isra brushed it away, laughing.

When she was born it was like the vulnerability I'd always felt when facing the world, when facing the cruelty of others, had finally found its target. I survived my childhood—my childhood as a black person in Sweden—only to find that she was the one who saved me. She saved me from the Rabbit Yard. Their laughter echoed between the buildings—she and Isra were having a snowball fight.

When the girl from Tundra left her hospital bed in Brussels that summer night, it was snowing. As far as I understand, researchers have dismissed the phenomenon as an oddity, an anomaly.

Maybe the coincidence meant nothing.

What did she want with me?

Who was I to her?

In her seminal work *A Cyborg Manifesto*, Donna Haraway wrote about science fiction—to which the girl's delusions perhaps should be counted—and how it was a "negotiation of reality." Remembering the pictures from al-Mima, I wondered if the girl's writing wasn't doing exactly what Haraway was talking about: finding a way of negotiating with the world that had hurt her so terribly.

4

Who knows how we eventually arrived at the Rabbit Yard. I don't know if we came by bus or car, or if we walked. I don't remember the gates or the color of the guards' uniforms. But I can tell you about the pork dished up every single day. Every single slice of sausage and cold-cut.

I'm writing to those of you who don't know yet that madness will always become normal; in the end, normality becomes madness.

On the day in camp we were shown the Amin video, we were given sandwiches, and the thin slice of pink pork on my bread was streaked with blood. It reminded me of flayed human flesh.

The dining hall was a former gymnasium filled with clunky furniture that could have been taken from parks or highway rest stops. An old basketball hoop was still mounted to one of the walls.

I remember Dad poking at his sandwich. He picked off a cucumber slice and the meat underneath had paled, like the skin under a Band-Aid.

We'd never eaten anything that had even been near pork before. We ate a few vegetables from the edge of the plate, if we could, or bread and jam that Dad got ahold of somehow.

It wasn't only for religious reasons, but more to have control over something. Yani #eatingdisorder.

My shoes squished when I got up: we picked the pork from our plates and threw it on the floor, so a layer of grayish, squishy meat built up under the tables and chairs. A bit of sausage from yesterday's lunch stuck to the tread of my sole, and when I dug it out with a plastic fork I was reminded of the man who'd been swallowed by a giant fish in the Koran, and who was stuck inside.

I thought: We're in the belly of Sweden.

We had daily classes in Building K, a yellow brick building that must've been a real school once, because there was a jungle gym and a paved soccer field outside. There were different teachers every day: one time it was a Swedish guy my age who talked about men having to change diapers and vacuum; the next time one of the guards put on a cartoon about how children are made—with sperm that were like little white submarines and stuff—and the next time it was something different again. The teachers called themselves "democracy entrepreneurs" and "free speech coaches" and "dialogue activists," and wrote their names on the whiteboard.

On that particular day our teacher was an older man with gray dreads knotted at his neck and lots of bronze and cloth bracelets. The head of a museum, apparently. He pulled down a projection screen, started the film, and sat in a corner of the darkened classroom, looking pained by the events on screen.

"Light," Amin said, and his sister turned on the cellphone's flashlight and pointed it at him.

He looked at me as he killed them. I felt an ache in my gut. Like I missed him or he missed me, and I shut my eyes but I still heard the screams and cries and chairs falling over.

I opened my eyes right as Amin's sister turned the camera on the shop door, where the police were trying to get in. Blue lights twinkled in the darkness, and when she detonated her bomb vest the screen went black.

I remember thinking that she and Amin had let the emptiness in and it made them strong.

The teacher switched on the overhead lights and rolled up the blackout blinds. That day, sand was blowing through the air, spring or fall. A patrol car was turning around on the soccer field outside. The teacher was going on about freedom of speech and the, you know, right to blaspheme. He showed us posters of Göran Loberg's drawings, which we'd all seen a hundred times already—in the citizen contract and at school and as everybody's profile picture each year on February seventeenth. Then he handed out paper and pens and asked us to make our own drawings. He said it was an opportunity to break the psychological barrier.

Dad drew a black man with thick balloon lips and charcoal skin. Others drew pictures of men with turbans and long, drooping noses. I realized that everybody was copying Loberg's pictures so their threat level wouldn't be raised, so I did too. Afterward the teacher put the pictures he liked best up on the classroom wall.

I get a lot of headaches. It's like my brain is being split in half. I sit in my room at Tundra and listen to the other inmates screaming. I look out at the falling leaves, the falling snow, the falling rain, and I know that what I remember was real, but also that the proof would be me not being able to say a single word about it.

The map of the Rabbit Yard is still burned into my retina.

During the first year, Dad and I were living in a striped

zone in one of the tall apartment buildings I'd seen when me, Liat, and Bilal drove out there. If our threat level was raised—which could happen if you wore religious clothing, were caught in the wrong zone, didn't cooperate in class at Building K, or had a certain style of beard, etcetera—if that happened we'd have to move to a checkered zone, which apparently meant we wouldn't have our own apartment—we'd have to live in a parking garage or gym. If our threat level was raised even more, we'd end up in a black zone: only allowed out on the open fields where the drones could film us, where maybe we'd find a burned-out car or an old trailer for shelter, or live in one of the hundreds of little tents a theater troupe had donated to the Rabbit Yard once upon a time—flimsy tents made of dirty neon fabric that collapsed when it rained.

The map of the various zones was on bulletin boards fixed to walls and put up on metal stands everywhere. White, striped, checkered, and black patches.

I don't remember my own name, but I remember that map.

I was standing by the window. Dad was at a rickety desk with metal legs, a photo album open in front of him; he was leaning over it and touching the dirty pages, wavy with damp and age.

People laughing into the camera.

He'd found the photo album when we were cleaning out the apartment: a child on its mother's shoulders; a woman wading into the sea, her smiling face in profile. Dad kept leafing through it. The mom and dad with their arms around each other. The child, alone. The family didn't look Swedish. But they seemed to be happy anyway.

I wondered if they were Swedish citizens who'd moved

away after the riots and everything, or if these were three of the many refugees who'd lived in the Rabbit Yard before it was turned into a camp for us.

I don't remember many living people from the Rabbit Yard, but there were thousands. I do remember the family in the photo album. Their dark eyes and laughter frozen for eternity.

I only remember the living as whispers, as shadows on the wall.

A power station made of giant metal discs piled high into towers and a number of drab brick buildings sunk into the last of the snow in the industrial area flew past the train window.

I went through my notes about the man I was on my way to meet, rereading the questions I wanted to ask and thinking about how to begin. I was having a hard time concentrating, the thumping of the rails was lulling and I'd been up all night. After a while I put my headphones on and shut my eyes.

A man was calling into a local American radio station. He sounded confused and disjointed, a black man going by his voice, maybe middle-aged, with a whiff of mental illness. He was talking about a group of children. They'd knocked on his front door one night, but ran away when he opened up, and later in the night they'd stood outside his bedroom window, peering in. Distressed, he said their eyes were like black holes leading to nothing.

I was listening to an audio file Isra had sent me. I'd started collecting testimonies about time travel and multiple dimensions, in an attempt to get an overview of the state the girl from Tundra was in.

I slipped between sleep and waking.

The radio host let the man talk, asking questions every now and again. The man claimed the children had asked for shelter from the cold and he'd let them in, only to be forced to "travel through time":

"Each time it happens I lose part of myself." His voice, which was nearly overwhelmed by the quivering frequency and atmospheric disruptions, sounded terrified—as if the children with the empty eyes were in the room in which he was speaking. "I had a family. But I'm lost in time now," he said. "I've lost them to time. I couldn't tell you what they look like anymore."

The conversation stopped. I slowly opened my eyes. Drifts of timber behind a fence. Logging machinery, claws and arms resting on the frosty earth.

The girl in the clinic claimed her consciousness had been sent back in time and somehow landed in Annika Isagel's apathetic body at al-Mima. For some reason she hadn't just gone back in time, but sideways, to our world, which was different from the one she'd left behind: in her world Amin's sister hadn't died, as had happened here. So she'd come here to take the sister's place, but also to stop the attack at Hondo's. This was just about as clearly as I understood her delusions. I wondered what it was in the human soul that surfaced as an idea about stepping in and out of time, as if moving between rooms in a house. Some sort of dream about nothing being definitive. Outside, post office terminals, roundabouts, and open fields passed by. Do I dare stay in this country? I wasn't just an origin seeking its future on the Western world's screens. I was carrying shards of another world, different grammar in which I ordered space and time. I was Muslim, and it was during those years that I started to think this made me a monster in Sweden.

The man I was meeting was waiting outside the Pressbyrån kiosk at the train station, smoking. He was around twenty-five and dressed in a blue warm-up jacket with the Italian national soccer team's emblem on the chest. We shook hands, went to the parking lot, and got into his red Mazda. We drove through town with the air roaring through the windows, which he'd rolled down because he was still smoking.

"I didn't think you'd want to meet me," I half shouted over the noise from the wind. He glanced at me, then turned his eyes back to the road.

The apartment was in a three-story brick building. The hall and stairwell smelled of dog or cat piss, and three girls who could have been in elementary school rushed by in their quilted jackets, taking no notice of us.

He unlocked the door, and led me into the hall. The stench of smoke hit me, as though something had caught fire, but it was only that the apartment hadn't been aired out. A studio apartment with a kitchen nook. Black leather sofa, an unmade mattress in one corner. The floor was piled with clothing and fast food containers, the place seethed with self-imposed isolation, like a sniper's nest. A Barcelona scarf was hanging on the wall. The man went into the kitchen, rinsed out a drinking glass, filled it with water, and put it on a coffee table covered with cigarette butts and soda cans.

"Have you prayed *'asr*?" he asked. The afternoon prayer, named after shadows stretched by time. I shook my head and we took turns washing ourselves in his bathroom and then prayed together. He prayed an extra prayer when we were done with the prescribed ritual. I sat on the prayer mat, watching him finish his bows and Koran recitations.

He was born in Sweden to Somali parents; had been arrested by American mercenaries during a trip to the south of the country five years ago; and was taken to al-Mima, accused of having been a member of al-Shabaab, which has been designated a terrorist organization. Unlike the girl, he'd been set free only when al-Mima was shuttered and razed.

The journalist from *Aftonbladet* had forwarded my request to him. I don't know why his reply had taken a year to arrive. When he was done praying, we folded up our prayer mats and sat on the sofa.

"So you're writing a book about her? The terrorist?" His hair was trimmed, his beard grew in tufts on his chin and cheeks. According to the article in *Aftonbladet* he'd never been a member of al-Shabaab, but had written a number of social media posts in support of them. More than anything, I think he'd called the girl from Tundra a terrorist ironically, playing with how casually the label was tossed around.

The sofa's dry, cracked leather groaned when I rearranged my legs.

I took out my phone, turned on the recorder.

"You could say I'm writing about what happened that night."

I put the phone on the table, but he took it, powered it down fully, handed it to me, and said:

"Yani, I can get into trouble." He made a vague gesture in the air. "They're listening, you know what I'm sayin'?"

If we hadn't just prayed together, I would've suspected him of having smoked hash or something—his movements were irregular and he was unable to look me in the eye.

If I couldn't record the conversation, I'd need a pen and notepad. Searching through the books and papers in my bag, I put a number of items on the table in front of us—among them, the latest installment of the girl's story.

"That's a lot of trash, brother."

"It's material for the book. Sorry."

He reached for the pile of papers, and because I couldn't think of a reason why not, I let him look through them.

I picked up my glass of water, took a sip, and said, "What did they do to you out there?" I didn't say the name of the place out loud. I've never liked doing it. *Al-Mima.* As if the sound itself had power.

"So what, you don't read the papers?" he hissed, and I couldn't tell if he was actually being hostile or just trying to protect himself from the shame he must feel because of my gaze and the information that had gone public about him. About his body.

"They did experiments on you. Tortured you. You want to talk about that?"

The way he was staring at a scrawl of smoke hanging in the twilight of the apartment seemed to say that every stone, every grain of sand had cracked in half. Instead of responding, he read the girl's account.

I'm writing to you because you can still be saved.

Liat's dad and I were sitting outside the gym he lived in with lots of other people, mostly white Swedes and Jews. Snow dusted the trash and gravel around us. I was sitting on a metal railing, blowing into my hands to warm them.

The office chair he was sitting in had no wheels and kept almost tipping over. He wiggled in it while unleashing blasts of moaning melodies on a trumpet.

"At first he didn't say anything, right?" I said. "He just stood there by his desk, panting." I was telling him about something that had happened in Building K that day during class. A guy had stood up and interrupted the teacher. "Everyone thought he was going to end up in the black zone, but then he started shouting about how he hated Islam and stuff. Distancing himself. And the teacher straight up started crying."

"Of course," said Liat's dad. He had a higher threat level than me and was on a different schedule, so he wasn't in Building K in the mornings.

"Wallah moron."

"Moron," he said, then made the trumpet whine. White

clouds of breath floated out with each shrill note.

The teacher—a woman with braided hair who was supposed to teach us the theory of evolution using pictures of ape-people and fish—had reported the guy to the guards, and his threat level was lowered. He was moved to a better apartment, in a zone with heat and running water.

"You know what those lessons are actually about, don't you?" Liat's dad asked.

"Learning stuff," I said, and he went serious, eyes drilling into me. He and Liat's mom had left Israel before Liat was born because he hadn't wanted to do military service there, and I think the light in his eyes had something to do with it. Not being capable of murder. He said:

"It's about making sure there are certain people who you can talk to in any way you please."

"Why?"

"Because then you can do anything to us."

A drone buzzed by. It was like a manta ray with small jet engines set in a sturdy, articulated aluminum frame; it turned its camera globe on us, and when we held up the small paper IDs with our threat level printed both in writing and as a barcode, it zipped off between the buildings.

"When I was like nine," I said, "Liat saw something online and decided we were going to be bombers."

"What are bombers?"

"Yani writers," I said, and when he didn't get me then either, I waved my hand around like yo, you're really going to make me explain it, but then I said it anyway: "Taggers."

"Taggers," he said, and grinned.

"Taggers," I said. "So we took our allowance and bought white spray paint at the energy station and started tagging walls and underpasses and everything."

"You were nine?"

"Nine or ten."

He fingered the trumpet, put it near his lips, opening and closing the brass valves, and said, "I think I know how this one ends."

"We got busted by security," I said. "They never took us in but they held us down and spray-painted our faces."

He laughed. The trumpet, which was pressed to his mouth, snorted and wailed.

"So that's what happened," he said.

"Yeah. What'd you think?"

He shrugged.

"Her mom said she came home with white paint all over her face. I thought she'd tried to make herself suedi."

Dad peeled off the slice of pork and threw it on the floor. He stared at his bread for a long time, then pushed his plate away and got up.

Classes in Building K about the positive effects of colonialism in the Third World, why the death penalty was justified in a democracy like Sweden but not in a dictatorship, and the importance of personal hygiene.

I remember spending hours staring at a spot of mold on our kitchen wall. I thought it was like a satellite image of a dark storm, and if I sat there long enough it would start to spin.

This was the second summer in the Rabbit Yard.

We stood in line for the water truck. One of the guards hit a guy in the face and I remember feeling completely calm, like it was no big deal, something that happened all the time. The guy who got punched—an Arabic teenager wearing an

Adidas jacket—screamed and fell to his knees, and the guard kept wailing on him.

I remember the dull buzz of the electric truck's engine. Those of us standing in line glanced at each other, but our gazes didn't reach all the way, they bent and splintered like fiberglass canes.

I got to know the guy later, even though I don't remember his name anymore. He had a friend, and their favorite thing was to sit in one of the doorways telling each other ghost stories. The one doing the talking would shine a flashlight on his face, doing voices and everything. Their favorite subject was what happened in Building T, which was a fenced-in five-story building where, like, social security and health offices and whatever had once been, when the Rabbit Yard was a normal suburb. Building T was on a hill, so its greenish copper face could be seen from almost anywhere in the Rabbit Yard, and I heard you ended up there if you got caught trying to escape. The guys said they experimented on people in there. They'd noticed birds didn't fly over it, and if guard dogs were forced to go inside the fence, they'd panic and bark themselves hoarse.

Whenever the Crusading Hearts came through they were armed with knives and iron pipes and sometimes they had spears or axes—there was usually one who was wasted and being laughed at and filmed by the others. Yani #swedishumor.

They always arrived in the evening or at night, and for the most part they stuck to the black zones, but one time Dad and I could hear them yelling and clomping up and down the stairs. We hid in the closet under a blanket.

We heard our front door open. They ransacked the

apartment, pushing over the furniture and kicking things.

People said the guards opened the gates for them.

A scream came from the apartment above, where a Swedish woman lived. She'd ended up in the Rabbit Yard for sheltering enemies of Sweden at home. I clung to Dad, hugging his tense, frightened body. It sounded like someone was dragging her down the stairs—we heard a series of dull, hard thuds.

The intruders in our apartment ran out into the stairwell. When I peeked through the crack of the closet door I saw the last of them leaving. She looked young, wearing a black jacket and white sneakers. She was taking a final look at the apartment. Our eyes met. A Swedish flag was tied over her nose and mouth. I remember her blue eyes.

My classmates had talked about how being a Crusading Heart was good for your career, yani that it looked good if you wanted to get into business or politics, so I don't think they were wearing masks because they wanted to hide their identities. They wanted to show us we no longer deserved to see them, in the same way the woman who'd examined us might have been wearing gloves because we no longer deserved to be touched by a Swede.

The girl stared at me, then turned and walked out the door.

I thought she'd tell the others about us and they'd come back, but that didn't happen.

Later, we crawled out into the clutter. Dad gathered his photo albums and put them back on their shelf.

"It's airborne," he muttered, apropos of nothing. He'd got it into his head that they were poisoning us that year, zapping us with invisible death rays or something. He smacked his lips. "You know the taste, right? It's like foil."

Sometimes the words we used with each other didn't seem to belong to our language anymore, they were just sounds being forced out of our throats, hollow sounds, like air whistling through a broken ventilator fan.

The ham had small holes where the meat mixture had set around air bubbles. As I took it off the bread Dad watched me, resigned, curious but indifferent. The light in his eyes was snuffed out. I threw it on the floor and brought the bread to my lips. It must have been winter already, because a few snowflakes were falling through a broken window high up in the dining hall ceiling.

I stopped myself from gagging and took a bite.

I didn't actually do it out of hunger. I did it because Dad was about to crack, and if he cracked, he'd cross a line and would stop being himself—my only parent, Dad who took care of me and taught me about the silence in writing through his own.

He threw himself over his bread. He even licked his fingers and ate each crumb off his plate, thinking he was saving me from what I was saving him from.

I pressed my forehead to the plastic tarp, which was thudding in the wind. It was toward the end of Ramadan and not many of us in the Rabbit Yard had fasted, but we had gathered in the soccer field to pray the special prayer that marks its end. We were using large tarps instead of prayer mats, because they were banned as ideological symbols. I sat up and felt the wind on my face and thought nothing in the world is like God and that's why God's power is fearsome. I prayed, without words, sitting with my hands cupped like a bowl, and sent everything straight up.

After, in the apartment, Dad took a clunky military-green

device from his pocket. He said it was a satellite phone that would work even though the web was blocked in the Rabbit Yard. Who knows how he'd gotten hold of it.

"I paid enough to talk for a few minutes," he said.

Liat still had the poster of blue-haired Oh Nana Yurg on her wall.

Liat's eyes were heavily done up, and she was wearing black lipstick, a retro look that was in, out there in the world. She leaned over her screen to get a better look, and winced as if something had frightened her. When I looked in the little window in the corner, where I could see what she was seeing, I understood why: I didn't look like myself. I looked dead. Wallah #zombie.

Maybe she said my name. Maybe she said, *Oh God is that you?*

"Have you seen my dad?"

"I miss you," I said, instead of answering.

Dad had left me alone by the kitchen window where the signal was the strongest, and it had started raining, a gentle shower hitting the peeling blue façades at an angle.

"I miss you too. You seen him?"

"Yeah, a few times."

"How is he?"

Her question told me she was still in a world where truth existed, even though she was living in a country that wanted her dead. I wouldn't be able to tell her about the threat levels, about the drones sailing over the collapsed roofs, about Building K or Building T.

There were no words for how any of us were doing in the Rabbit Yard. Liat and I looked at each other through our screens. I thought of Amin, also looking into the world through a screen, from a place on the other side of everything.

"I'm running out of credit," I said, because it was less of a lie than anything I would've said about her dad.

"Can I call you? Can you add me?"

"That probably doesn't work on this phone," I said. "Bye."

I sat by the window. Alien. Looked down at my hands and thought strings and ropes were running under my skin. A Jew, a Muslim, and a beggar walk into a bank. Have you heard that one? What do you call a Muslim in a dress?

I shut my eyes. We had been born in Sweden without being Swedish, and that made us unreal. Only by dying would we become real again.

I logged into my old Sensly account, where I still was a regular brown-haired Swedish girl. I wrote a hit list. Five best things about Mom. Number five: she was strong. So strong. Four: she was the best in the world at listening to me talk about my problems in school and stuff, and about what I thought about the world. Three? Three was her smile when she talked about God and how God's light shined right through her. Number two: her way of teasing dad, which made the whole family laugh until it hurt.

I sat in the window, typing on the satellite phone's large, clunky keys.

Number one was how, when I was little and couldn't sleep, she used to tell me stories, and how on lots of nights I still whisper her words to myself, in her voice.

He put his cigarette out in an empty soda can.

"What's this?" He'd finished reading and set the papers aside, far from him, nervous and troubled.

"She wrote that."

"The girl who tried to blow up the comic book store?"

I nodded, said, "She was in al-Mima while you were there."

"I heard." He knocked another cigarette from the pack, spun it between his fingers; I think he was trying to center himself after having been drawn in to the girl's story. He mumbled:

"At first it's like, no way are they going to hit you. Cuz you're Swedish." He laughed at that last bit, then put the cigarette between his lips. Let it hang there, unlit. "Yani, a Swedish citizen."

Again I was thinking he looked dazed or high. I wanted to ask him to crack a window, but I was afraid of changing the subject now that he'd finally started talking about al-Mima.

"They hit you?" I asked. He lit the cigarette.

"Hit me," he said, nodding formally. The cherry crackled as he dragged on the cigarette. He seemed, in some indeterminate way, even more crazy than the girl from Tundra. "And they had machines, you know what I'm sayin'?" he said. "They stuck cables to your head, brother."

I wanted him to explain how the girl had learned Swedish. I wanted to know why she didn't remember her real family. What had happened to the prisoners at al-Mima? What did she want with me?

"It was like getting zapped with electricity," he said, "the hairs on your arms stood straight up, you know what I'm sayin'?"

"Yes," I said, taking frantic notes on his way of being and articulating himself more than the story he was telling, which so far I recognized from other accounts of al-Mima.

"Then you got all dizzy and couldn't remember your name and shit. It was like being stuck right at the edge of sleep, brother."

I came to think of a phrase the girl had used to describe how memories of the future surged in her at Hondo's: *like waking from a dream.*

But nothing had to mean anything.

"Then you started remembering stuff." He glanced at me. "Crazy things, brother." He stifled a cough. "Yo, I was lying there with the cables and everything in my head, remembering how I'd driven a car full of explosives straight into a building in Mogadishu."

"When?"

"That's the thing, brother." His front teeth were chipped, the chips showed whenever he laughed—a serrated row of shark teeth. "It never happened. But I remembered doing it." He shook his head as though denying the whole experience, driving it from himself, then lifted his hands, rubbed his neck, and whispered in a way that suggested he didn't really believe himself either: "I remembered doing it in the future. I'd exploded."

He put his head in his hands. Time passed. Then he looked up at me, searching for something. Trust? Understanding? He sucked his broken teeth with a scowl that maybe meant he was trying to reconnect with what had been wiped out. "I can't explain."

"The girl said she remembers things from the future, too. She doesn't think she's the same person that was taken to the desert. She thinks she comes from another world. Another time."

"Swear. Say *wallah*," he said. After I'd assured him I wasn't lying and explained that the account he'd read was the girl's testimony, what she claimed to remember, he told me—fumbling and ravaged—about what had happened to him in al-Mima. It was in this smoky apartment in depopulated central Sweden that I realized the girl wasn't alone in her illness. Her madness and its specific expressions had come from al-Mima: the victims had somehow made sense of the torture with the help of fantasies about it being a gateway to other times and lives.

The blinds were pulled down and as the man was speaking, darkness fell and the streetlamps lit up—their cold light filtered into the room in straight lines.

She's kneeling. She's wearing a hood; they put it on her during the flight. She has no idea where she is. They arrested her on her way home from school. It's possible that's when she tried to resist, or it was whenever the guards tore off her clothes and dressed her in the orange jumpsuit. It's possible she tried to tear herself free when they shaved her head.

Maybe she's already bruised.

She tells them she's a Belgian citizen, first in Flemish then in English.

I know this because it's what any of us would shout into the dark. I'm a citizen, there are higher powers watching over me.

Maybe she hears men laughing at her pleas, at her naïve and archaic credos.

I wonder if she's panicking, if she feels like she's choking.

Maybe she saw a hazy strip of light under the black fabric as she was being led between the airplane and car under the vast, stark desert sky, and could tell by the shade or intensity of the colors that she wasn't in Europe anymore.

They pull off her hood.

There are masked people in front of her. In the room

is a yellow plastic bucket, a faucet, a bench. A video camera. Simple objects transformed—now threatening and thick with violence. A drain covered by a moldy plastic grate. Metal rings attached to cement walls. Even the sand along the baseboards—everything has a barren quality, full of potential pain.

A place beyond the world. Or at its center.

She asks what they want with her. She even starts rambling about her willingness to cooperate, which she hopes will assert her innocence: all they have to do is ask and she'll tell them anything, but the masked people stay silent—I imagine they're letting the terror of silence saturate the room.

Along one wall, near the steel door, are black metal cabinets, which several witnesses take to be computers. One of the masked people goes to them, rolls out a bundle of white electrical cables and fastens them to the girl's shaved head with suction cups. Fans inside the cabinets begin to whir. She is still kneeling; she feels dizzy, breathes fast, the hairs on her arms bristle. Absolute zero. After a while she realizes she can't remember her name. Terrifying. She doesn't remember who she is, where she comes from, or how she ended up here. She's searching for a reference point, for a foothold in the scraped-out, filthy room, in the masked faces, the expressionless eyes. The dull sound of the fans in the large computers makes her think of a washing machine or an airplane engine, or of a large predator, or maybe of nothing in particular.

Maybe she's thinking: like being stuck right at the edge of sleep.

One of the masked people gives her strange instructions:

"I want you to empty yourself." Several victims recount these words. "Empty your consciousness."

Presumably she nods, obedient and jittery.

"I want you to try to remember specific things. Can you

help us with that? Try to remember someone who has the black flag with the emblem on their clothes or in their apartment. Do you know it? Daesh's flag?"

Maybe she tries to interject—she'll give them names right now, on Facebook some of her boyfriend's relatives and friends have the flag as their profile picture—but she gets cut off. "It might be a Muslim who practices martial arts. Try to remember stuff like that. Muslims who removed themselves from society, who might have weapons at home. You might even be the one doing these things, do you understand? Try to remember."

She nods at this last part, unsure what the words mean.

You might even be the one.

They strap ski goggles blacked out with paint and headphones on her. A hollow, unmodulated crackle is playing.

They leave.

Time passes. Hours, days. Noise and darkness. Darkness and noise. Emptiness.

Maybe she's connected to a drip and medical personnel are furnishing her with catheters.

Sometimes a damp rag is squeezed into her mouth.

I looked up into the snow falling over the courtyard.

A tremor runs through her, like an animal twitching as it dreams, and she makes small sticky and fractured sounds.

I looked through the peephole. It was dark out there.

She's disembodied, like she doesn't really exist anymore.

When they finally take off the headphones and the blacked-out ski goggles, she turns away from the bulb in the ceiling and screams as though she's been kicked hard between the legs.

For a long time all she can discern are gray shadows, gray light. Her ears have gotten used to the crackling in the headphones and voices sound rough and uneven.

"What did you see?"

She leans forward and thick vomit spills across the cement floor. No sense of identity, no solid core.

Who is she?

This must be what it's like to witness your own annihilation.

"As this was happening, did you ever feel like you were someone else?" I asked. The Swedish-Somali took a drag on his cigarette, squinting in thought.

"I don't know. I remembered things that were going to happen. Things I was going to do in the future. But I think I was still myself in all of those memories." He started fiddling with the cigarette pack on the table, shoveling the ash and dust around, drawing a few meaningless characters, and repeated: "I don't know."

Toward the end of the conversation he told me something that would become key.

A few times during his stay in al-Mima he was taken from his cell to a room where he was put in front of a screen and asked to study film clips and photographs. Veiled women and bearded men with long jallabias crossed squares and train platforms. Black-and-white, low resolution, jerky sequences captured by security cameras. He scanned through passport photos and private pictures from cellphones, relaxed, often joyful in a way that felt creepy when seeing them there, in that room in the desert. Young men with their arms around each other in a mosque, or with expensive cars.

An archive.

The masked people asked him if anyone in the pictures, anyone at all, was going to be with him when he was blown up in the future.

"I didn't recognize anybody," he told me. "But I pointed sometimes."

I took notes, I felt empathy, I wanted to hug him, or at least touch his arm as he sat there wrapped in cigarette smoke, isolated from all that is human.

"You know why I did it? Why I pointed people out?"

"Because otherwise they'd have hit you?"

"They hit me anyway. No, it triggered the memories, somehow," he said, and scratched his shaved head. I wondered if he laid awake at night, if he had a hard time differentiating between his actual memories and the strange hallucinations he'd had in al-Mima. He said: "I did it because I knew I was in the desert because someone else had been there before me, sitting in that same chair and looking at that same screen. Some other Muslim had seen my face and pointed at it."

We crunched along a narrow gravel path. The girl was wearing a thin jacket and chunky pink plastic sandals. It was our first meeting outdoors. She'd given me another stack of paper, which I'd put in my shoulder bag. At this point I'd accepted that her account, more than anything, was a way to get me to keep coming back to Tundra. I might have been the only person not getting paid to see her.

"If it's possible to stop the genocide by stopping Hamad and Amin," I said, "what does that say about hate?"

We were in the park surrounding the asylum, I had my

cellphone out recording our conversation.

"What hate?"

"The hatred people feel for those of us who are not what you call Swedish. The people in the Rabbit Yard in your story. What does that say about the hatred of us if the future you remember was prevented just because you stopped the attack on Hondo's?"

In the past year, two books of reportage on the attack had been published. One focused on the mistakes that had been made during the police response—starting with the shot fired at Hamad, which went completely against the Swedish police's standard procedure in a hostage situation. The other book contained a few of the hostages' stories, notably Christian Hondo's, who also talked about his store, its history, and the philosophy behind it.

A movie about the attack had been made by a new production company.

"If what you're telling me is true," I said, "then they hate us only because of what we are or are not doing, and it has nothing to do with the people who hate us. You're letting them off the hook, because you're saying their hatred was a result of the attack."

She shrugged at my logic. Whenever I looked at her, waves of something like love washed over me. I would've wanted to get to know her beyond the fence, outside all of this.

Maybe it was a sign that I was now as lost as she was.

"I met a man who was where you were."

"In the Rabbit Yard?"

"In al-Mima," I said, and she let out a disappointed laugh.

"Oh yeah?" She scratched her head, she had a boy's haircut. It's possible the orderlies had given it to her because it was easy to maintain. It wasn't the first or last time her head was uncovered during our meetings. I don't know if this necessarily meant anything special.

"You don't remember a room where you sat in front of a screen showing pictures of other people? In al-Mima? Pictures from security cameras and passport photos and so on."

She shook her head, suddenly suspicious, she said, "Why are you asking?"

"The company staffing the prison, and that tortured you and the others who ended up there, seemed to have access to some method of planting false memories—and possibly entire fake identities—inside people. And for some reason they wanted to connect these with real people by showing the prisoners pictures."

"How do you know?"

"I suspect it's so," I said. "I don't know anything."

Insects rose and dove around us. The park wasn't very big and we kept passing the same trees and bushes on our walk.

"I think the beatings and the water torture were just a way to create the stress needed for the method to work."

"Well I don't remember any room with a screen." Walking along in those ugly plastic sandals, she snuck a look at me.

But this must've been where you saw Amin for the first time, right?" She didn't answer, she didn't really seem to know how to orient herself in this conversation. "It must've been why you recognized him on the streetcar, right? Might it even be the reason you came to Gothenburg?"

"Maybe," she said. She wrapped her arms around herself. I could've hugged her right then. The terrorist from February seventeenth. The Belgian Black Widow. I wanted to embrace her. I felt sick, on the verge of going crazy. She went over to a blooming bush, heavy with white roses like knotted lace, squatted down, and gingerly lifted one. Something in her way of crouching aged her; she was like an old woman in her garden at the end of life. She looked like Mom.

"Do you feel hopeful?" She asked this without looking up at me. I was taken aback both by the question and by the fact that I didn't have an immediate response. I was one step behind her and felt the heat from the brick wall on my face. She continued, "Hopeful about Sweden? About life with your family here?"

A weight dropped through me. When a minute had passed without me answering she changed the subject. As though to spare me.

"Amin had mad skills with mopeds." She laughed at those words and her innocence even made me smile. "One day he took apart his 180. I mean, before the attack and everything, when we were just two normal people, you know? He took the motor apart, chain, transmission, everything. Laid it out in the courtyard. Then put it back together again exactly like before. I took pictures. He was planning on sending them to a garage." She changed her voice, mimicking a young man's, the accent stronger than her own. It was Amin speaking, through her mouth: "Yo, after they see these pics, they gotta give me a job." She squinted thoughtfully into the light, at me or the sky.

I would have wanted to protect her from al-Mima. From the torturers and what they turned her into.

A bee buzzed by; she watched it go.

"Bees were smaller in my time," she said. "As small as fruit flies. They'd done something to their DNA so that they wouldn't die from pesticides."

Would she ever leave Tundra, would she wake up one day

and remember what happened to her in the desert, and her parents, her life in Brussels, her language?

The thought frightened me more than anything else.

"We learned about it in school," she said and dropped the white flower, letting it fall to the earth.

The black hood covers her head. She can make out the ceiling lamp through the dark fabric—a dancing beam of light pushing through the darkness.

They arrange her body so her head is tilted back and put something else over her face, something heavy and cold that intensifies the dark and molds to her cheeks, sinks into her eye sockets. It's just a wet towel. They're pouring water on it; it's running down her chest and through her hair, going up her nostrils and seeping into her mouth. Her body quakes, arms and legs shaking wildly.

She's trying to hold her breath as hands press down on her chest, slow and business-like, forcing the air from her lungs.

Bursting pain.

Animal panic flooding her mind.

Who is she? Why are they doing this to her?

She breathes in; can't help it. She wants to stay in the light and heat—she inhales the ice-cold water.

Here is the hollow core.

Here is where she begins and ends.

The intersection.

Why does she remember a pig's head among shards of glass? A man who stashes books under his mattress? The dark water runs into her lungs and the world narrows into a strip, seconds expand into extinguishing days, years.

But in another world.

In another time she's in another place.

She isn't here.

My toes sank into the wet sand. Isra and I were carrying our shoes, the wind was blowing through our clothes and carried with it the smell of rotting seaweed. This was in the summer, before our daughter's school started up again and we'd booked a room at a hostel just outside of Halmstad for the weekend. She was playing in the waves, collecting shells and stones in a plastic bag; Isra and I were ambling under a turbulent August sky, full of shrieking gulls and sardine clouds.

The summer ripened then reached its end, in those years as ever.

"She asked me if I felt hopeful. About Sweden."

"What did you say?"

"I didn't have an answer."

Isra was quiet; I was quiet. We caught sight of a structure a little way off and wandered in that direction. A group of teens were just beyond it, they might have been drinking beer or making out. A bare cement cube, half buried in the sand.

"Why would a military contractor plant that story in her?" I wondered. "About Sweden? About a future where Muslims are annihilated by fascists?"

Isra looked at me, worried, disappointed.

"What is it about her that draws you in? Why can't you just let her go?" She'd flipped through the girl's papers and listened to the recordings of my visits to the clinic; the magnetic power of the girl from Tundra evaded her.

The feeling that one time our fingers touched.

Interwoven.

I didn't reply, Isra said, "If she really started to have doubts about the attack—why didn't she leave? She must've had plenty of chances to just open the shop door and walk away before the weapons came out. She could have left and called the police."

"She thought she recognized Amin and Hamad. From her real life." I don't know why I was defending her, only that I had to. "But really I think she'd seen them on a computer screen at al-Mima."

Our daughter shrieked as she ran along, the waves roaring onto the land and crashing into white foam. Now and then she picked something out of the sand and put it in her plastic bag. Tiny, simple, holy things, salvaged from what to her must resemble God.

But God resembles nothing.

The building was just an old bunker, a fortification left over from the Second World War—probably part of what had been called the Skåne Line, built as a defense against invading Germans. The roof was overgrown with beach grass and the concrete was graffitied inside and out. A memory from a war that never reached us. A future that had existed only in the minds of military strategists.

"Do you remember Jamila?" Isra said. I nodded. A young girl Isra had taught to recite from the Koran. Lively, intelligent. Played tennis. Tunisian parents.

"Her older brother went to Syria last week," Isra said.

"To Syria? Why didn't you say anything?"

She didn't reply, and her silence made me feel guilty, as though my meetings with the girl from Tundra betrayed something between me and my wife.

"Their mother can't stop crying," Isra said, and I tried to imagine what it would be like to lose my own child to Daesh, to that suicide cult the movement, after the most recent military defeats, had unarguably become.

“They will drown in their mothers’ tears,” Isra said. “Those who go there to die. In the next world.”

The gulls screeched overhead.

“Maybe we should move.”

“Where? To Algeria? Like in that girl’s story?”

“To my sister’s,” I said.

“Toronto?”

“Why not?”

“Because of what she says about Sweden? Do you believe her?”

I shook my head firmly and gave a laugh, short and then severed.

Sometimes I thought that night had yet to end: Amin still had Göran Loberg in his grasp, ready to slice up the world with his little box cutter, and let the darkness in. That’s why I had to write the book. To resist him, like the girl from Tundra had done.

I peered into the structure. A few centimeters of mud covered the floor and it smelled of urine and saltwater. The rough concrete was cold and scarred. I felt something moist. Jerked my hand back. Blood? Red spray paint. It must’ve been from those kids ahead of us up the beach. A geometric shape that looked like a rune. Hard to make out in the twilight of the bunker.

The angular metal pin stuck in it, like a snowflake crossed with a swastika.

Against the light I searched for the kids, trying to see if they were Swedish. If Swedes would call them Swedish. I shouted to our daughter to come join us. Shouting that the world is less safe than the sea.

And the Xerox-pulse of blue light sweeps through the store, moving soundlessly over Amin's pallid face, over the triangular blade of the knife, over the overturned and scattered comic books.

Outside the megaphone blares. *Talk. Talk to us.*

I'm writing to those of you who won't believe that what I'm saying can happen in Sweden. You'll think I'm lying because you still think you're Swedish.

The bluish smoke from the shot-down drone was bitter and burned my eyes as I pushed my way through the crowd.

People were clapping and singing. Amin, something, Amin, Amin.

The image on the rain-splattered paper someone shoved in my hand was faded. His face. A still from the Hondo video and something in Arabic I couldn't make out.

A young guy with a black-and-white striped soccer shirt was standing over the smoking wreckage and talking excitedly while waving a homemade weapon, which I assumed he'd used to shoot down the drone, a tangle of duct tape and steel pipes and plastic. The drone's fins and camera casings reminded me of something that had evolved in the ocean over millions of years, or an exercise device you order online to get buff biceps.

Amin, sang the crowd, Amin, something, Amin, Amin.

His gaze, warped and blurry. His eyes, recognizing me.

The black zones in the Rabbit Yard were stormed that night. From our window, Dad and I saw the security company's bulldozers and armored vans crashing through the tents and trailers. In their riot gear the guards looked like large insects working in the fiery thunder of spinning emergency lights, spraying tear gas and using blocky, nasty weapons that shot violet blinding flashes: people who got hit put their hands over their eyes and threw themselves on the ground, flailing.

Wallah, Star Wars.

A few days later Dad and I were taken aside on our way into the cafeteria. A guard confiscated our ID cards and issued us new ones using a tool hanging from her belt; our threat level had been raised. I think it was my fault, maybe they'd gone through the security footage from the crowd by the shot-down drone and spotted me.

We were banned from the striped zones. Dad asked one of our neighbors to bring us what was left of our things from the apartment, and we squeezed into an old grocery store where lots of people were already living.

I don't remember how long we'd been living in the Rabbit Yard then. I don't remember if we talked to the people we were living with or if we kept to ourselves. I still thought about Liat sometimes: how she was doing and what she'd been doing since finishing school. Dad couldn't get ahold of insulin anymore, and his eyes bled—ugly reddish yellow marks flaring like sunspots on the whites. I talked to him about trying to leave the Rabbit Yard, because sometimes people did climb over the fence into Sweden, even if lots of them were arrested and ended up in Building T, never to be seen again.

"Dad," I said. "There's no life here."

He listened halfheartedly, paging through one of his photo albums, but instead of answering he took a closer look and squinted, as though it wasn't me, but the family in the pictures talking to him.

He didn't say a word when we walked through the cafeteria. He would pick the ham off the bread or out of the pasta sauce. His shaking, tired hands would guide the white plastic fork to his mouth and carry his silence the same way a conductor's hands can when they've stopped the music.

I started visiting the area where the drone had been shot down, wandering among the trailers and burned-out cars. Sometimes men hollered at me, threatening, yani *come here* or *what you doing here. Sister. Yo, sister.* Flyers fluttered in the mud. Some people were calling themselves *The Martyr Amin's Holy Warrior Brigade*—they must've run an Arabic phrase through some bad translation program. It must have been them who handed me the paper in the crowd by the shot-down drone. I even found pages with poems on them, short verses about fire and paradise, which I folded up and saved.

After a while the women started greeting me, even as they pulled their veils around themselves more tightly, hiding their features.

One evening, the air smelling of trash and dusty earth—a smell I associate with summer in the Rabbit Yard—I thought I saw the Arabic guy who'd shot down the drone and who I was sure had been taken away, but when he turned around I realized it was just someone else wearing his black-and-white soccer shirt, a North African, a few years older than me, with mussed dark curls. He was hanging around a tent with his friends, who noticed me looking at them. They pointed and laughed, but then muttered something in Arabic, scolding. There was something searching in the way he moved, and when he turned to face me I saw that his eyes were pale and cloudy, and the skin around them was burned—a strip of wrinkled flesh across his cheeks and forehead—he must've been hit by the weapon the guards were using.

"Dad. It's death here. We can't stay."

"Death does not exist in the world," Dad said. "Death is inside us."

Top three things I missed about our last apartment… Number three was a working toilet. Since moving we'd only used the porta-potties that had been put around an old square and that didn't get emptied often enough. I mean total balagan. Two: having a door to close, so I could be alone with my thoughts. Number one was the window, where I could sit and look out. All the windows in the grocery store were covered with plywood and taped-up cardboard. Maybe that was why I was almost never there, because I felt shut in.

I got to know a group of women who cooked watery soup for people in the black zone. They reminded me of the bearded brothers who'd come to the last mosque, and I ended up with the job of collecting and washing the plastic dishes. I started mimicking their speech and their modest way of covering their mouths when they laughed, and was let inside their tents and trailers, where I sat with my legs folded under me, listening. They belonged to a group who believed that liberation would be ours if Muslims gave up *dunya*, yani this world, which wasn't actually real anyway.

You know, Sufis, like Mom.

One of them had worked as a journalist before she ended up in the Rabbit Yard. She was a Somali woman, the most beautiful person I'd ever seen in my life wallah. She'd found a printer in a school and dragged it to a trailer where they connected it to a cellphone so it could print out poems by

Rabia Basri, a Sufi saint I knew about because Mom talked about her sometimes.

I think that was my third summer in the Rabbit Yard. I was looking for a home or a way out. It might have been three years since Mom's death. Dad cried often, silently, his mouth ajar, his hard face wet with tears.

"Dad. If I leave the Rabbit Yard, how will you manage?"

His silence, I thought, was how the emptiness screamed.

I walked through those mild nights, over the fields littered with cars and trailers and tents. Rabia wrote that she carried a torch and a pail of water so she could burn down the gardens of paradise and quench the fires of hell, because she wanted people to pray to God for God's own sake. The women made fun of me because I was unmarried, laughing behind their hands flecked with ink from old broken toner cartridges.

Dreams about Amin, still.

"Amin?"

"Hamad."

He was sitting on a bed with me. He held his hands like a machine gun and shook them silently.

I woke up in the grocery store's oppressive dark. A car drove by outside. By the time I got dressed and was at the door, another one passed by. Trash and dry earth whirled around the tires. I went out into the dusty night. The machines were at work off in the distance.

They were using shipping containers to build a wall outside the fence.

I sat outside the store on an upside-down milk crate and watched the sky brighten. The morning was unusually peaceful. When we got to Building K for our lesson, which had been changed to the morning since our threat level had been raised, it was locked. Something was wrong. There were no guards anywhere and no lunch was being served. I saw shadows in the windows of Building T, high up on the hill, but otherwise the entire Rabbit Yard seemed to have been abandoned by anyone who wasn't locked in. By the afternoon, after I'd spent hours trying to get through to Dad, he said, like he was talking about someone about to repaint the walls in his apartment:

"They might firebomb us."

In the evening trucks arrived and men and women with white surgical masks climbed atop the containers and threw in large white sacks of rice.

I visited the women. They were sitting outside their trailer. One of them said there had been a terror attack in Stockholm, another said she'd heard the Swedish military was going to attack the Rabbit Yard in order to train for an overseas mission, the third said it was all a cost-cutting measure.

I remember a shirtless man. He had dark fungal boils on his chest and walked around the square, screaming and pointing at them as if they were signs of the infidels' evil or marks that God had made in order to elevate him to king.

I don't know if the Rabbit Yard had been blockaded for days or weeks or longer, but the first deaths happened that night, and the next day during the burials panic spread, as the size of the death toll sank in.

We hid in the shop for a long time, it could have been weeks.

I remember my hands running over my skin, terrified of every little speck of dirt and scratching at my birthmarks until they started to bleed. I remember crumbling up a slice of bread and feeding the crumbs to Dad.

When I headed out in the morning it was quiet, like the whole world was underwater or in a glass case. As though the emptiness had finally taken over the Rabbit Yard.

A guard stood on one of the containers and, instead of keeping out of sight, I stood below him, waiting for him to look at me. I wanted to be seen by eyes that did not belong to those of us who were locked in here. But the visor of his helmet was pulled down. It shimmered a little when he moved his head.

I heard a whining sound, either a man praying or a barking dog.

A forgotten line of laundry stretched between two apartment balconies fluttered in the wind.

I remember a corridor full of flies and a woman, her face covered in scabs like a mask of dried clay, who said the company in charge of the Rabbit Yard was allowing us to be used as guinea pigs for new medicines, and that's where the plague came from.

At some point the blockade must have been lifted, because I remember new people arriving in buses and the lessons in Building K starting back up.

The dead were buried in the soccer fields.

I know you don't want to believe this can happen in the country where you and your children are living. My parents didn't want to either.

But the Rabbit Yard was in Sweden.

In the mornings the blankets we'd wrapped ourselves in were covered in ice crystals. I spent my time with the women in the black zone; I wanted them to keep telling me about God's wrath, about how the earth would one day quake and throw up the dead, about how the angels would drag people behind them on iron hooks on the Day of Judgment.

One day, a pair of them were outside their trailer, hands bound with zip ties, and the journalist was kneeling in the mud and trying to wrap herself in a blue veil with gold embroidery, which a dog kept pulling off her. The guards around her were laughing and filming with their cellphones.

The printer came flying out of the trailer door and smashed to bits.

My head was resting on Dad's chest. The sound of a patrol car's electric engine accelerating away between the buildings faded.

"What is it you see in those pictures?"

When he just kept lying there staring at the ceiling, I opened one of his photo albums. The mom was posing for a portrait. Her child was in her arms, they were standing in bright light by the wall of a red house.

I thought the Rabbit Yard was the ground they were standing on, a patch of earth in the midst of everything normal.

I touched the photo hesitantly.

"I'm listening to their faces," Dad said.

I inspected the woman's lips, the spots on her skin, eruptions of sun and joy.

"What are they saying?"

"Thou shalt not kill," Dad said, using the old timey words, but then reflexively he rephrased it for me: "It means you're not supposed to murder people."

His chest was rising slowly, hissing under my head. He

must've guessed what I was going to say, I'd said it so many times before after all, because he asked, "Where would we go?"

"Away from here."

I put the photo album down, and joined him in staring up at the moldy, cracked ceiling.

"Do you remember her face?" he asked. I knew he was talking about Mom. When I closed my eyes I could see the creases around her eyes when she smiled and how she'd reach out and brush my cheek. The ocean's roar.

If I'd been a real poet, like Rabia or the blind woman from Iran, I wouldn't have to write all of this down. It all feels like lies anyway. I would've been able to write a poem and hold out each word one at a time, showing how broken they were in my time, how they were like the rest of the trash strewn in the Rabbit Yard.

Words like old refrigerator doors and bricks broken in half, words that were no good for anything, words like the innards of cars and washing machines. Buckled, rusty words, words like punctured hoses and torn clothes and rugs, words you wouldn't touch unless you were wearing gloves.

I left Dad.

I remember my jacket ripping as I climbed over the fence and the guards chasing me into the abandoned shopping center where I hid among clothes racks and broken mannequins. I remember the plastic body parts all around me, and the dogs' claws clacking on the shop floor as they came to find me, and that they just stared at me, tongues wagging.

Then how they went quiet and retreated.

I remember having become someone whom even dogs were afraid of.

I hid in the old shopping center for half a day, and then struck off across playgrounds and school grounds, through the long shadows. Two children were kicking a ball against a wall, and it seemed unreal that children could still play.

If I'd written a poem about everything, I would've used the melody from a song I'd heard a group of women in black singing during a burial when the plague was at its worst. A Kurdish or Persian tradition, where they walked in line behind the bundle of cloth that was to be buried. They screamed. Screamed as if they could wake the dead. Screamed until their voices cracked.

Screamed because they had survived.

Yellow leaves blew around my feet. I took the routes where I thought I wouldn't be stopped by Crusading Hearts or guards or ordinary Swedes. They were playing the video of Amin again. He was watching me from billboards and bus stops.

A light was on in our living room window. Where else would I have gone? When I drew close and peered in I was almost surprised to see a Swedish family sitting there instead of me, Mom, and Dad. A car passed by on the road past the playground, the sound made me jump and cower.

I was a memory, a refugee.

Liat's window was dark. I climbed up the drainpipe. The height didn't scare me. I knew there was danger in normalcy, in happiness and safety.

The apartment was empty. It wasn't even furnished anymore.

Like we'd never existed.

The two empty swings nearby swayed in the wind. Top five nice things Liat had done for me. Number five: protected me from annoying boys. Four: taught me to dance like Oh Nana Yurg when we were nine.

Over by the bus stop Amin was pulling Göran Loberg by the hair. I swung faster and the wind dried my tears. Liat and I had been a part of Sweden that wasn't Sweden, a part the country around me needed to be able to cleanse itself of.

We had been Sweden's dead skin and long nails.

The screen went black, the text said that everything could've been different, if only the Swedes hadn't been so kind, Hondo's would never have happened. The video started again, Amin taking out the knife, sliding out the blade. I didn't notice when the guards arrived. Too tired to run. Now that Liat wasn't here anymore, I wanted to be back with Dad.

The guards were wearing yellow hats with brown lettering, which meant they belonged to the company that handled security in the neighborhood—some of my old neighbors must've seen me in the swing and called them. I didn't have my passport with me of course, they checked my eyes with an app, locked me in the backseat of their car. They'd parked by the bus stop and the LCD screen's light flickered through the window, onto the tattered seat, over my hands. After a while a car came from the company that ran the Rabbit Yard and I was transferred.

We followed the outer border. Night had fallen and it was raining, again I saw the fences, apartment blocks that had gone up in flames, the misty rain on the car windows looked like hairspray. We pulled into a garage under Building T and one of the guards took me to a changing room where a towel and a gray sweatsuit were laid out on a bench. I showered and changed, and two other men, dressed in white, came to get me.

They locked me in a room where a guy with a shaved head was sitting on a mattress. He was staring straight ahead, like he was inspecting the cracks in the paint on one of the walls. It took a minute before I saw who it was.

I sat down on the empty mattress. He said, "As-salaamu-alaikum. I'm Bilal." He didn't seem to recognize me. Liat's old boyfriend, the one with the cauliflower ears and beautiful eyes who'd been so in love with her that summer when we were still in the midst of life. I hadn't noticed him in the Rabbit Yard so he must've come to Building T from a different camp, or straight from the streets.

"I knew Liat," I said, but he didn't understand. He ran a trembling hand over his shaved scalp.

"Who?"

"I'm Liat's best friend."

He wrinkled his forehead and said, "Shit."

I thought about what I'd imagined: the black hole in the middle of the Rabbit Yard. That's where I was now.

"So you just got here," he said.

"How do you know?"

"You still have your hair."

5

She was staring through the fence at the pale, stubby grass on the other side.

"Where are you going?" The voice was a hoarse whisper. She looked older, in that timeless way you sometimes see in the institutionalized—on her way to becoming an overgrown, ancient child.

"To Canada. My sister lives there."

"When?"

"It's a long process. We have to organize visas and work. A place to live. It won't be for at least a year."

She nodded curtly. Sometimes I wondered how the crushing sorrow she radiated squared with the notion that she'd escaped a fate that, according to her story, might have been worse than death. In her mind, hadn't she stopped everything she was writing about from happening?

There was a change in her energy—maybe an indistinct shift in her posture.

"What are you thinking about?" I asked, and she turned her attention to me, squeamish, as if the sound of my voice had surprised her. She took a step back, seemed introverted and nervous. Something had happened to her face, her expression—it was like a different consciousness was inhabiting her nervous system. Her curious illness.

I asked her if she was angry, and she turned away, back to the fields, to the grass and sky. She kept sneaking frightened, wary looks at me, and after a minute or so I thought I saw her change again: shoulders drawn up in her usual crooked way; the band of panic stretched tight across her eyes vanished.

If I'd known her real name, or if like Amin I'd given her one of my own, I would've said it.

Another minute passed.

"Sometimes I'm that other girl," she said. "The one they say I am. Annika."

"You remember your real life?"

She shook her head, slowly, like in a fog.

"It's not like that. Who I am now, the person talking to you, disappears. It started happening like a month ago. I slip away."

"Slip away?"

"You know, like when you fall asleep or whatever. I don't exist anymore. Then I come back. Sometimes it's been a minute, sometimes an hour, sometimes longer, and I know she's been here, in her body." Her laughter sounded distressed. "Balagan," she sighed.

The word, which recurred in her account, was modern Israeli slang. Maybe it wasn't strange for her to be using it: she may very well have been friends with a Jewish girl before she was sent to al-Mima.

"Sometimes I remember things after she's been here," she said. "Like when a window stays fogged with breath after someone's been standing there looking out, you know?"

On a gravel path behind us the Bear Man passed by with a guard—I turned, because I didn't like having my back to the

Bear Man. Both he and the guard were smoking and speaking softly to each other.

"Do you remember anything now?" I asked when they were out of sight.

"I remember a woman who played with me, and a few words in another language."

I was full of misgivings. I didn't want that—what had happened right then when she hadn't been in my world—to happen again. I felt dizzy.

"Yani, Belgian," she said.

"Flemish," I corrected, and she put her hands in her pockets. Something seemed to rise up, then sink inside her.

I wanted to ask her to describe the symbol the fascists had used in her future, to compare it with the one the kids had painted at the beach last summer. But then I would've been giving into something.

Everything was wrong.

"Lately, they've been showing clips from the video to justify shutting down the Öresund Bridge, did you hear about that?"

"My video?" she said. "From the comic book store?"

I nodded. "Big demonstrations and counter-demonstrations down in Malmö."

"I have to ask you something."

"Ask."

"I know you're gonna say no."

"Ask."

"Can I meet your wife?"

"Isra? Why?"

"Please," she begged in a childish tone that was new.

"But why?"

She couldn't answer, and the question ran into the sand.

What did she want with us?

Everything was wrong.

A flock of birds had been scared out of a tree on the other side of the fence and was circling it, a shrieking dark ring.

We sat on the rug in our living room, twelve people in a circle, a *halaqa*: men and women gathered to forget the world for a while, scarves wrapped around their shoulders or draped over their heads, crocheted kufis or baseball caps on backward, hoodies and jallabias, one sister who'd come straight from work was wearing a bus driver's uniform. Isra was carrying around a dish of incense, the sweet sandalwood smoke rose to the ceiling. We'd moved the sofa out of the way, the chairs and table were against the wall to make room for it all; I was holding my daughter, and when we began the evening's *dhikr* she mimicked me as my inadequate voice called for the Unparalleled, that which carried our souls in His open palm. Allah. I rocked back and forth, eyes shut. Her higher-pitched voice within mine. Allah. The windows were open to the cool fall evening and under our chanting voices the sound of traffic and shouting teenagers died out.

Was the girl from Tundra the reason we couldn't stay here? Were her words what was driving us to leave my mother's grave, the communal laundry rooms, and the trees lighting up in fall?

Nothing in me was freed from the world's forgetfulness, nothing remembered that this world was not mankind's home.

When we had finished our dhikr and prayed, my daughter stayed in my arms, and like me she cupped her hands and whispered into their bowl.

She and I had tried to save a magpie's life earlier in the

week: our cat caught it and left it on our balcony and we gave it scraps of food and water and then buried it together. We'd even read a passage from the Koran, crouching by the flowerbed. She was at that age where not one day would pass without her tugging at me, eagerly pointing out a cloud formation or the opalescent shine of a beetle's shell, and I didn't know what she was praying for there in my lap, because I imagined she was already in paradise.

Make me true, I whispered and looked down into my own palms. Cupped, the lines and folds of skin were like the facets of a crystal.

Turn my body into a question.

Forgive us.

After tea, the guests left, brothers and sisters dispersing under a darkening cover of clouds.

We'd told them about our plan to leave Sweden. Mido had tried to convince us to stay, others understood, harboring similar plans.

Down in the courtyard Mido turned to me, up on the balcony, and waved. He put his hand to his heart.

Were we birds?

Have mercy on us.

Put light inside us. Light around us.

Two teenage girls were smoking in an entryway across the courtyard and what could I think of if not her. She, Amin, and Hamad were liminal beings, caught mid-transformation. And therefore monstrous. They'd gone around with their machine guns, through the blood spatter and scattered comic books and toys, screaming about God and the Prophet. I thought they were the monsters of the Reformation, without really knowing what I meant by that. An image from the war came to me. Where had I seen it? A jihadist had gotten hold of a tank and was tooling around on a street. Like a child skidding her bike on gravel.

Amin's mother was waiting for me in a café on the square in Hasselbo. I'd been trying to reach her, via various mosques and trying my luck with phone calls, when suddenly she'd picked up and agreed to meet.

At the table next to us, a group of older Arabic men were drinking tea, dressed in suits even though it was a Tuesday afternoon. They were loud and jolly, and made her—hunched over her coffee in a fluffy gray winter coat, hair in a bun at her neck, bent by an incredible weight—seem like she was on a planet where gravity exerted a stronger pull.

Amin's cousin, a few years older than what Amin would've been, sat next to her and seemed sulky even as he wolfed down his cinnamon bun. I recognized him from a couple of articles I'd read. I don't know if she'd asked him to join her for our interview or if it had been his idea.

I greeted them, bought a cup of tea, joined them.

A biting cold day, a bluish whiteout rolled over the cement slabs outside the café window.

The cousin asked if I was a journalist. I said I was a poet and author, which he didn't really seem to relate to. He was wearing a white polo shirt and a blue cap, faded by sun and rain. A string of numbers was tattooed on his neck. Later I found out it was the zip code of an area in Borås where he'd lived for some of his childhood—you could find out a lot about him, and the rest of Amin's family, on racist web forums.

"What do you want to know about Amin?" Amin's mother asked. When I told her that it was up to her, she took a photo out of her handbag and put it on the table's crocheted lace cloth.

The picture had been taken outside, on a patch of grass with a cement wall in the background. A boy, maybe three years old, was holding an infant. It had to be Amin and Nour.

"He had a lot of love in him," she said. The cousin shifted in his chair and made a face that suggested nausea, rage, and also maybe a measure of healthy suspicion for yet another man who wanted to write about their dead. "A lot of love," she repeated, caressing the photo. The little girl. "Do you know what happened to her? To Nour? Has anyone told you?"

"Only what I read in the papers. She died. An accident."

Of course there had been articles about all of this after the attack. Most of them painted her as quite a terrible mother—a welfare case, irresponsible, a parasite, even though she'd been working at various old age homes and as a personal assistant since she and her husband had arrived in Sweden in the late '90s.

The accident, Nour drowning in the bathtub, was painted as suspicious in the most speculative reports—a sign of the darkness that had come to haunt the family.

"Look at all the love."

"Yes," I said, and it was like her fingertips had burned to the waxy faded surface—her hand was shaking but didn't leave the photograph. "He only left her in the bathtub for a second," she said. "Amin's dad. He just wanted to see the news." She couldn't stop staring at the picture, her face twisted into a searching and tormented grimace, as though she were loosening a knot tied tight inside her.

"It was about the war. In our country. He just wanted to see the news."

"About Iraq," the cousin interjected.

"About Iraq. He just wanted to see what was happening back home as it was being bombed." She made an evasive gesture with her free hand, and said: "He couldn't stay with us after that. He lives in Norway."

She told me about Amin's childhood, about his dreams of working at Volvo on Hisingen, about him drifting ever further away from the family over time. During our meeting she was often on the verge of tears, and when she did cry, the cousin put a comforting hand on her shoulder. I don't know why, but it surprised me—because of who I thought a young guy from Hasselbo with a neck tattoo could be. Toward the end of our conversation he tilted his head to the side and looked at me, eyes narrowing, sizing something up, and said:

"I tried to tell him. Brother. This life you're living, brother, it's nothing." He shook his head. "Running the streets. It's nothing."

The article I remembered him from included some of his criminal record. He had, like Amin, been found guilty of several petty crimes: in his case carjacking. Most recently he'd been involved in credit card fraud, he was the one referred to as "the goalie"—that is, the one who let his face be caught on the ATM machine's security camera. He'd probably owed somebody money and they'd forced him to take part in the fraud. He spent a couple of months at a facility in Helsingborg and was let out about a month before this meeting.

Stray January snowflakes blew across the square and collected in a thin white line on the wall of a hair salon. He repeated:

"It's nothing."

I looked at him and thought: *Love mistaken for weakness.*

"Did you notice when Amin started becoming interested in Daesh?"

Amin's mother picked up the photo and carefully tucked it into her handbag.

"I noticed his eyes change. And that he stopped smoking hash." She snuffled and laughed and gave me a self-conscious look. "A mother knows."

"Did he ever talk to you about it? About Daesh?"

She fumbled with the brass buckle on the bag.

"Once, I think. I was surprised to hear him talking about Islam at all."

"Excuse me, but aren't you Muslims?"

She opened her hands and said, "Alhamdulillah. But he didn't like religion. He didn't want to listen when I tried to talk to him about God, about him bettering himself, about *Yawm al-Qiyamah*."

"The Day of Judgement," the cousin translated, and even though I knew the Arabic term, I thanked him with a nod.

"He thought we were dumb. Muslims. Backward. So I don't know how he got it in his head that he was going to do jihad." She smiled when she said it, a pure and honest smile, like a camera flash, quickly snuffed out, leaving a sort of soot in her eyes. She stirred her coffee. "But he brought the girl to my house once. The girl who killed him."

"Tell him what she told you," the cousin said; she shook her head—a movement that resembled the cousin's gesture when he'd talked about the streets—like she wanted to shake something off that was stuck to her, tangled in her hair.

"It was like they were playing, you know? They were pretending. He said her name was Nour. But that's my daughter's name."

"Tell him what she said," the cousin repeated.

"She told me that I shouldn't have pictures on the walls. Can you imagine? She's my guest, and she's saying angels won't visit my home if I have pictures on the walls. She's telling me to take the pictures of my girl down."

I nodded, wanting to offer comfort, but I couldn't find the words. I looked at the square and remembered my childhood in similar places. It could've been me out there freezing by the newsstand, full of rage directed at a country I didn't think acknowledged my humanity, and running around the streets at night. Reaching for something shimmering deep inside the fights and flexes with my aching, bruised hands. Scribbles of ink on the surface of a world that would never be mine.

The Rabbit Yard.

I got ahold of Göran Loberg and interviewed him over Skype one spring evening. The internet connection on his end was bad: he was either overseas or in some remote location in Sweden.

"A young man is holding a box cutter to your throat," I said, and the video stream froze in a low resolution, pixelated portrait of him. "Are you still there?"

"You're wondering what I was thinking?" his voice said, floating around my kitchen.

"Exactly."

"It was quite a long and drawn out situation. I was angry, of course. I was worried about the wound in my leg, where one of them had shot me."

On the screen he was mid-gesture, sitting in front of the white plaster wall, bare-chested for some reason. His face was grooved and the reflection of the computer screen in his glasses was like a neon blue chip.

"Hamad," I said.

"Right. Then they were disagreeing about something, too."

"What can you remember about it?"

"The young woman was having some sort of psychotic break, I think. By then I was probably too shocked to be following along." His cough was wet and rattling. "Please excuse my being in bed," he said—it hadn't occurred to me. "I have a hard time sleeping at night."

"Because of the death threats?"

"Maybe." The video stream came back to life again, and from another coughing fit he'd collected phlegm or a blood clot in his mouth, which he sucked on and dissolved, smacking it like old people do. He swallowed it with a bitter look and cleared his throat. "Whatever the case, I'm not sure my thoughts are what's interesting in this situation."

I was at the table, outside the streetlights shone on frosty sandboxes and steaming laundry vents, single snowflakes sailing past what should have been safe.

"So what's interesting, then?"

"The role of the girl, of course. The idea of giving death meaning by filming it."

According to his blog, which I visited before our interview, his latest work was about filming the dying at a hospice, a concept that, prior to this exchange, I'd read as a return to a type of art he'd done early in his career, when he'd explored time and death, in more or less dogmatic forms—for example with illegal sculptures that posed a hazard to the public.

The shadow on the wall behind him was bluish, and I sensed something barren and dismal about the place he was in: a hotel room or some other impersonal dump furnished so it could be left in a rush.

"What do you think about when you lie awake at night? May I ask that?"

He scratched his chest hair and his hoarse laughter triggered a convulsive coughing fit, more phlegm came up, and he smacked at it again in order to choke it down.

"About how the hours pile up like driftwood," he said. "Shapes in blowing sand. I've begun to understand that time is an organic membrane that lays itself on top of things." He scratched a scab on his forehead. "Maybe time is no more than a film of skin cells on a pillow in a hotel room where an artist, marked by scandal, is hiding out for a couple of nights," he added, with a self-mockery that made me feel some sympathy for him.

He picked a dry flake of skin off his forehead and looked at it.

"Nowadays it's the racists who are taking the place traditionally occupied by artists," he said, a notion, a thought that came from sleeplessness. "That is to say, today the racists are the provocateurs getting people into a carnivalesque mood." I wondered if he'd brought this up to reassert the distance between us.

"Is that how you came up with the idea for your comic book?"

He looked incredulous.

"I wouldn't say that."

"How did you get the idea? Do you remember?"

Of course, I had a copy of the book somewhere in my office, but I rarely opened it because the pictures disgusted and hurt me.

"I was flipping through the cable channels one night," he said. "Floods. Sports. Porn. And then those pictures from Iraq flickered by. Abu Ghraib? Do you remember them?"

"Of course."

"I'd seen them before, but that night I was struck by—shall we call it a philosophical notion? A man with a dog collar around his neck. People piled up like pyramids." He looked invitingly into the webcam and reached for some indistinct shape in the air in front of him. It reminded me that he'd spent years teaching at an art school in Gothenburg. "What torture does," he says, "is put the body on some sort of stage. It shows that nothing but the body matters. Right?"

"Maybe," I said, not because I didn't understand the logic, but because I didn't necessarily want to be drawn into his world of ideas.

"Torture shows how impossible it is to have a body while imagining there's anything to ideology, religion, culture, right? Torture shows the tortured, and everyone else, how ridiculous it even is to be creatures made of flesh and skin and nerves who allow themselves to believe that some things are holy. Do you follow?"

"I'm not sure," I said. He sighed and seemed to be deciding whether or not to elaborate.

"What I'm saying," he said, "is that I was on the sofa one night and saw those pictures on CNN. A man smeared with feces, for example. And I couldn't help cracking up, you know? Do you understand?"

I didn't know how to react. I changed the subject. The interview went on for no more than another half hour, we talked about his childhood, the place of freedom of speech in Enlightenment ideals, and various comic book artists we had both read and whose work resonated with us.

A couple of times I noticed his left hand start shaking as he tried to force it into a fist but his fingers refused and cramped up like a claw, which he then tried to bind with help of the other hand—he would busy himself like that for a while, almost automatically, but each time, when he realized I was watching him through the webcam, he dropped both hands. I wondered what it meant. I studied his aging body in the computer screen's unforgiving light. After our conversation he'd still be lying there thinking about time, about what it was. If it was anything more than a dark speck of dust and dead flies collected at the bottom of a bathroom light fixture.

I asked him if he thought our mortality made us human—an attempt to push past the academic surface of the conversation and reach something else—but he just laughed at the question. By then he'd taken out a roll of paper towels and was spitting the phlegm into a torn-off sheet.

"What should I have asked instead?"

"You should have finished thinking that through," he said. "If death makes us human, then what does art do, art which makes us immortal? The picture stuttered and his gravelly, disembodied voice said: "Does it make us inhuman?"

The speakers crackled. His face had frozen again into a pixelated mask.

The minaret rose like a finger pointing to the sky. A couple of teens stood outside the mosque, stamping their feet to stay warm as they handed out free cash cards to those of us pouring out the doors—some sort of marketing campaign. The people I'd just prayed with passed me by and headed for the parking lot or the bus stop. I shook some hands, I watched their flapping jallabias and scarves, various head coverings, all of these signals, all that shimmering fabric, all the many interpretations of the world. Images turning like leaves in the wind.

Only by dying would we become real again.

Were we images?

A video in which Hamad executes a row of men, their hands tied behind their backs. He is masked and shoots them in the back of the head one by one. The media got ahold of and disseminated the video after the attack on Hondo's. Presumably filmed in Syria, the buildings in the background are damaged beyond recognition.

It's raining, drops collect on the lens—spidery gray clusters of light that seem to wander across the screen—a hand wipes them away again and again.

Isra came into the office and stood behind me.

"I couldn't sleep either," she said, absently massaging my shoulders.

A jihadist behind Hamad holds up a black flag, it's soaking wet, looks heavy, as if it's made of iron, obsidian.

I'd just pressed play on the video for the third or fourth time. Hamad stands with his pistol pressed to the back of the first prisoner's head. Something happens before he pulls the trigger. There's a hesitation, like he doesn't really want to go through with it. The pistol wavers from side to side and he wipes rain or tears from his eyes.

He squeezes the trigger. The man in front of him collapses in the mud. As he moves on to the next prisoner I pause the film.

"I just mailed the copies," Isra said. She was talking about the scanned copies of our tax returns, which the Canadian Embassy needed for our visa applications. She was hoping to get a job at a university in Toronto as part of an exchange program, and my plan was to keep publishing books here in Sweden, even though I'd been feeling blocked lately.

I rested my head in my hand, not taking my eyes off the screen, and said, "Sometimes when we meet, I see the great darkness she's carrying. Like she actually comes from..." I couldn't finish the sentence.

"The future?" Isra asked, and as she said it, I heard the

madness that had crept into me unnoticed.

"Not from the future," I said. "But from a holocaust."

Isra sounded pensive.

"James Baldwin and Audre Lorde were in conversation once," she said. "Baldwin said something about the American Dream, that both Martin Luther King Jr. and Malcolm X had believed in it, in spite of everything. Something like that. Then Audre Lorde said no one had dreamed about her ever, not once. No one dreamed about the black woman except to figure out how they would eradicate her. When I read the girl's account I wondered if that's what it's like for Muslims in Sweden today. No one but Daesh dreams of us."

On the screen, Hamad still had his pistol raised. The rain was suspended around him, like silver light, a shattered mirror.

Isra went back to bed, but I stayed put. I wondered what dreams were being dreamed of me.

The Hondo film. I clicked on the sequence where Amin was laughing. Through the balaclava, his eyes looked happy, if touched by madness.

Göran Loberg had seen the images from Abu Ghraib and al-Mima and laughed.

Why was a man standing on a stool with electrical wires fixed to his groin and nipples? Maybe the answer was "Because it was being staged, because someone had a camera." Maybe the film was reason enough, maybe the film was the precedent for the events.

Why put a dog collar on a Muslim? Why was a man, dressed in a sweat-stained T-shirt, riding a naked Muslim who was on all fours? There's an answer that allows us to forget the question: These things happened because they thought

Muslims were ridiculous. Laughable. On-screen Amin was still giggling, but he was shaking his head and even gently stomping his foot.

First came the unbelievable; then the guffaw.

Maybe that's what Göran Loberg's drawings were expressing, and maybe that's why I experienced them as being so violent, even though they were mere strokes of ink.

I propped my elbows on the table. Felt sullied by the light of the screen. I started crying. I was seized by an incredible longing for Toronto, which I hadn't visited since my daughter was born. I longed for the city's chestnut trees, the sycamores in Rouge Park, for my sister, in whose face I could still see Mom.

Amin stared at me from the screen, laughing.

In Abu Ghraib, and maybe also in al-Mima, the victims were forced to partake in the production of the very images that made the violence possible. The gaze was a necessary part of both the torture and the terror attacks. My gaze. I shut my eyes, hard.

A war in which the gaze, our most tender touch, had been weaponized.

Amin laughed.

Why is a soldier building a pyramid of living people? Why is a prisoner being smeared in feces?

Isra would say that we were living in a time where every stone in the world had witnessed enough human cruelty to burst into shards.

I remembered something the girl from Tundra had written, about how the Rabbit Yard was the place from which they spent all their time looking out at Sweden, and that was why they hadn't seen the camp. Something like that. The camp had been invisible, because it was right beneath their feet.

I'm writing to those of you who have never existed.

I'm writing to you, to whom I have always written.

Me, who doesn't exist either.

My pulse sounded like it was hammering underwater, like it was echoing against the white-tiled walls, wet and distant.

"Do you speak Swedish?"

The blond man dropped a white sheet of some paper-thin material over my shoulders and fastened it tight around my neck with a strip of tape.

"Yes."

"Good," he said.

Something that sounded like a drill started buzzing behind my back, and I jumped, but it was just hair clippers. They tickled my temples and I watched my black curls fall in tufts.

"What are you doing?"

"You can have a veil, all you have to do is ask," the man replied. I don't know if he seriously thought he was answering my question or if he was just making fun of me. When he was done he took a tablet from a shelf and started asking me if I had heart problems or epilepsy or migraines, stuff like that.

Then I was in another room, its window facing the Rabbit Yard, the expanse of it beyond this enclosure. I remember looking down on the red broadleaf trees along the bike paths and footbridges, and I saw the apartment building where Dad and I had lived when we first came here.

"Can you let my dad know I'm here?" I said, but the woman who was with me in the room now—broader in the shoulders and older than the man who'd cut my hair, but with the same polite manner—didn't respond to that. She said:

"Please lie down here."

The hospital bed was surrounded by machines that had white plastic casings, and an IV-stand was hung with bags of translucent liquid in various colors.

"I didn't get sick."

"Excuse me?"

"I never had the plague," I said. "When people died." The woman laughed softly.

"That's not what this is about. Don't worry. Just lie down here." She patted the bed, and when I finally obeyed she stood at its foot, strapping my legs down with plastic straps.

"What are you doing?"

"Your arm, please," she said mildly, then strapped my wrists to the metal bedframe. I told myself that maybe she just wanted to protect me, that she wished me well. When she was done, she left the room and in the silence, the wet rush of my hammering heart returned as I tried not to panic. A detergent-like smell pierced my nostrils. Footsteps overhead died away.

I remembered the guys who'd said that dogs were scared to death of coming near here and birds didn't want to fly over this building.

The sheet I was on was made of the same papery material

as that man who cut my hair had used, and it rustled as I twisted in the bed and tugged at the straps.

Mom used to say the sound of the human heart was God's name.

Allah.

Help me.

Allah.

The door opened. The woman came back in. She switched on the machines, one by one, and pulled out a bunch of wires with suction cups on their ends. She stuck them to my forehead and shaved scalp. I pulled harder at the straps, and she hushed me. She took out a long needle and brought it to my left arm. I said, "Please," I said, "I'm sorry I escaped." I remember the needle straining and stinging my skin, then she connected a tube from one of the drip bags to it.

She left the room and later, after a few minutes or maybe as long as an hour, she returned with a man dressed in white, who carefully flicked the drip bag with his index finger.

"Can you contact my dad? Can you tell him I'm here?" My mouth was dry, my lips stuck to each other. The man ignored what I'd said.

"Right now we're giving you a medicine that inhibits motor function," he said. He was a pleasant, fit Swede who actually reminded me of a handball coach Liat had had a long time ago—the more I stared at him, the more I was convinced it was really him. "Do you know what it means to inhibit motor function?" he asked, and the tubes brushed against my skin when I shook my head.

"It means soon you'll notice that you can't move," the man said. The liquid ran through the tubes, pale red, like raspberry juice. "And in a second we're also going to administer a nerve toxin. It will feel like your entire body is burning." The man said this with total calm, and I wanted to scream but my mouth wouldn't move, it had stiffened half open and only a faint moan escaped from my throat. I could feel drool spilling from my mouth, down my chin.

"Clamp," the woman said, and out of the corner of my eye I saw the man take a shiny spoon-shaped object from a drawer, which he then stuck in my mouth. It had the icy bitter taste of stainless steel and clamped my tongue into place against my lower jaw. At the very least they wanted me to survive. The worst of my panic dimmed a bit.

"We'll start with fifteen milliliters a minute," the woman said, and even though my eyes were locked at a point on the ceiling, immobilized, I could sense the man touching the drip bags above me.

The pain came fast, spreading up my arms, along my back, and out into my body. It was a raining void, rays of nothing.

I lay on my mattress. Bilal studied me with a gaze that both pitied and abandoned me. Wallah, the way a security camera would look at you if it could feel bad for everything it had to see. I sat up and leaned against the wall. When I spoke my voice was hoarse.

"Why are they doing this?"

Bilal had been killing time by picking bits of foam off his mattress and lining them up in a long row on the floor. He pulled off another grimy yellow grain and said, "Knowing why only makes it worse."

To eat, we were given steamed vegetables and a spongy, grayish-purple cube that could've been meat or fish or anything. The soft plastic cutlery would barely cut the cube, and when I mentioned this to Bilal he ran the white knife across his throat to show you couldn't kill yourself with it either.

Sometimes I washed myself in the aluminum sink and prayed at what I thought might be the right time, even though it was impossible to tell since there were no windows. They took Bilal when the lights were off and we were sleeping. He fended them off listlessly. The room was eerie without him, like being alone in the dark with wild animals nearby. I remember wringing my hands and I can't explain how my knuckles and tendons frightened me.

They shoved him through the door a couple of hours later and I pulled his limp, feverish body to his mattress and carefully laid him out there. There was love, I noticed, in sitting next to his unconscious body and caressing his shaved head.

When he woke up they'd turned the ceiling lights back on and we'd been given food, which had already gone cold. He ate anyway, potatoes, carrots, and that purplish-gray meat or whatever it was, everything cut into strips. "They're recording it," he said.

"Recording what?"

His hands shook and he kept spilling his food, which I picked up and put on my empty plate.

"They're recording the pain and saving it. That's what the tubes and machines are for," he said. "They use the recordings when they steer their drones. Yani, the military and all."

"How do you know?"

"A Swede was in this cell when I arrived. One of those activists, right. She told me." He gave up trying to put the food into his mouth and feebly pushed the plate away. "They send signals to pilots, but upside down, like one of those, you know, what do you call them? Negatives. A negative. It makes them feel like they're really flying up there, over the desert. Like they don't have bodies, you know what I'm saying?"

He backed up, leaned against the wall, and said: "I told you knowing doesn't help."

I asked what happened to the Swede who'd been here before him, and he said, "She told me something else. Something I have to tell you."

"What?"

"The third time they do it, you die."

I stood at the window and looked out over the trees, whose leaves had fallen, knocked off by the rain.

"Go ahead and lie down here."

That time it had been a man, maybe one of the ones who'd taken Bilal in the dark, strapping me to the bed and sticking suction cups to my head.

I'm trying to remember the pain so I can describe it to you, but it's just a white shine, it was like winter sun flashing in puddles and broken windows in the Rabbit Yard, when I used to stare out the window, before.

Top five things to do while waiting for them to come get us for the last time. Number five: tear foam crumbs off the mattress and arrange them in a tidy row. Four: stare at the wall with #madpanic. Three: whisper God's name, over and over, to try to push away the pain still in your limbs like ice in your teeth. Number two: listen to the sounds from the vent, then hum the exact same sounds louder and louder until Bilal stares at you and cracks up. One: talk about all the crazy things Liat did.

"I taught her to drive, did you know that?" Bilal said once when we were doing thing number one. "We drove to the parking lot at the Mål of Gothenburg one night. Right over there, you know what I'm sayin'?"

"She told me. Said she had mad skills."

"Driving? She sucked." He laughed softly, fell silent, then used his sock to sweep away the line of foam crumbs.

Things happened in Building T that I haven't wanted to write about. Like when I was taken away the second time a cleaning cart in the corridor started rolling toward us all by itself, and the two guards who were escorting me stopped. The cart slowed down a few meters away from us, turned, and started rolling back so quickly it flipped over and crashed into a wall. Greenish water spilled across the floor. The guards didn't move a muscle and each held one of my arms. It took like five minutes before they dared go on.

One time when the ceiling light turned on, those foam crumbs Bilal and I used to fiddle with had arranged themselves in a wavy or swirl pattern. It would've taken hours for anyone to have set them up like that, and Bilal swore on his mother that he hadn't done it, and anyway it happened in the dark.

I think these things were related to the experiments they were doing on us, and because time was breaking down.

Balagan.

Bilal flipped out when they came to get him the last time. He backed into a corner and shook his head.

"Bilal. It won't help." The man who knew his name was tall and had scarred sunken cheeks—a guard I hadn't seen before. Bilal hunched as though he were seeking shelter from a strong wind blowing through the room, and I remembered how once I thought that Dad's hands cupped in prayer were like a fortress.

The man waited by the door, they were in no rush.

"Come on, Bilal."

Bilal was looking for something to cling to and latched on to the toilet bowl. His shoulder blades moved under his T-shirt as he wrapped himself more tightly around it, until the man with the scarred cheeks finally stepped into the room and started prying him off. They tussled for a while.

This is an image from the place I come from: a man clinging to a toilet bowl because he doesn't want to die.

My daughter was transfixed. I was holding my breath so as not to scare the deer, and carefully bent down so I could whisper in her ear:

"It's a love poem." Words that just came. The deer had dashed past the screen at the bus stop. It was twilight, no traffic, I felt reverence, sanctity; I was holding a grocery bag, it rustled and the animal jerked to attention, looking right at us with one eye. "A love poem from God," I whispered, and with a few stilted bounds the animal vanished into the woods. From the sidewalk, my daughter looked into the bare trees and shadows.

"Is every deer a love poem?" she wondered aloud. I thought about how open she was to the power of language. I asked her to take a seat at the bus stop.

"Are we going somewhere?" She was dangling her feet. Sweden was not at war. We were not being annihilated in death camps. Yet Isra and I were preparing to go away. Our visa applications had been accepted.

"Yes," I said. "We're going to take a trip."

"On the bus?" she asked. She didn't know she was about to leave her preschool, these seasons, this entire landscape.

She was about to leave her childhood behind.

"We're going to take an airplane to another country. Where my sister lives."

"Now?" she asked, shocked.

"No. With Mom, of course. But then we'll live there."

She looked toward the forested area across the road where the deer had receded from view.

"Is it because we're Muslim?" I nodded curtly. Then I realized I was letting her inherit my mother's fear.

I visited Tundra twice that spring. The first time we mostly talked about the year the girl had spent with Amin before they met Hamad. During our second meeting, on a day in March when a snowstorm had rolled in over the clinic, she'd almost exclusively channeled the part of herself that didn't recognize me, and might have been responding to something inside herself that was starting to remember her true self. I tried talking to her in English, but she withdrew and stood in a corner hugging herself, staring at me from some lost place within herself. I knew these episodes were signs of her slow recovery—the doctors had also mentioned it in an email—but when it happened I felt an inexplicable, devastating sorrow, because it meant that the girl I knew, the girl who was writing down her strange story, was disappearing.

Ramadan still came that year too. We gathered at the large mosque in Gothenburg to pray the final prayer and afterward there were balloons and treats for the children. Our final Ramadan in Sweden. Our friends had started to say goodbye, even though the trip was still far off. Mido tried to convince us to stay, he said there was still hope, and Isra and I were needed: if we couldn't stay in Sweden neither could he, and he and his family had nowhere else to go. But our decision had been made. The movement that began as a tremble in my body one fall evening years ago, when I first read the girl from Tundra's pages, had found a direction.

Still, something about her remained unresolved. A thorn in me.

When you said you were moving away, I was happy for you. I don't have any memories of Canada from my future. That's a good thing, I think. But I'll miss you. Then again there's so much I miss. In a way I miss myself most of all.

I don't remember the last time they strapped me to the bed. I remember a voice talking about not being able to drive home if the snow kept coming down like this. I pulled at the straps and prayed to God. I turned my head to the side so I could watch the snow falling outside the window, falling down over the dark mouths of the subway entrances and over the soccer fields that had become graveyards, and for a moment it was like it was falling upward, backward.

Someone caressed my forehead. Maybe because I was crying. I saw a moth. It was crawling over the drip bag, as large as a child's hand, and then flew at the window, toward the falling snow.

6

Brussels, early June, eighteen months before the attack on Hondo's. The hollow din of a power drill echoed in the hospital's parking lot. An ambulance driver was dangling his arm out the open window and trying to set the radio, which kept picking up some sort of disruption—a strange bleeping—he was swearing as he jumped between frequencies.

People coming through the automatic glass doors were gasping in the heat, fanning themselves with free magazines, grimacing at each other, and panting like dogs.

As a security guard, a Tunisian immigrant, was heading for the bus stop after her shift, her eyes fixed on a point somewhere out in the blue.

Did she think she was dreaming?

The news had reached inside the hospital, too, and patients and personnel alike made their way to the windows; they stood in their near-identical outfits, with their hours heading into overtime, afflictions, and IV-stands.

Their hands like pale starfish stuck to the glass.

It was June and it was snowing.

The phone rang at reception and the woman who picked up heard a series of drawn-out wails, which sounded to her like a signal picked up by a radio telescope, an atonal whale song from deep space. She sat, phone in hand, looking out through the glass façade at the snow falling harder, whirling along the curbs, melting into streams that flowed into the sewer, and then a gauzy blanket spreading across the ground.

Every telephone within about a kilometer's radius of the hospital started ringing and continued to do so for minutes. Those who answered heard the same strange wailing, modulating signal.

A group of teens on mopeds stopped and jumped off; they stretched their arms out and spun around, children once more.

A taxi driver who'd just dropped off a patient removed his shirt and knotted it over his face. He walked around tugging at people, trying to bring them to their senses.

"It's an unknown wind-born substance, take shelter you idiots," he said in broken Flemish. "Tomorrow morning, you'll be looking into your bathroom mirror holding clumps of your own hair."

An old man with a walker was catching the snow on his eyelashes. A woman in a hijab was having a snowball fight with her husband at a bus stop, laughing into the snowstorm's beating, confetti wings.

A clear plastic tube was below her nose. She stood at the window a long time, trying to access something important, someone who'd been important to her. A deep sorrow moved through her, a feeling of it all being too late, that this was already after the fact. She steadied herself with her drip stand. It was snowing, and without really knowing why, she started crying.

A man and a woman sat at the edge of the bed, speaking emphatically in a language she didn't understand. It was the day after the snowfall. She was having a hard time concentrating on their words and gestures because she sensed a threat at the periphery of the great nothingness that had taken possession of her. She didn't know who she was or where she came from. The man and woman were saying—this much she could understand from all their pointing—that her name was Annika.

An ordinary woman and a tall man with dark thinning hair, both vacant yet sullen. The man handed her a passport, and she read the name. Annika. She couldn't recognize the person in the photo.

After they left for the evening, she went to the window. Annika did. She wondered about the snow she'd seen. How could it be a summer's day. The face she'd seen in the mirror resembled her, but belonged to someone else. Annika.

The man and woman came several days in a row. They'd left the passport with her, in a dresser in the hospital room, and they kept taking it out and pointing at it during their visits. This is you. She wanted it to be true. She wanted to have a mom and dad. But she didn't think she did.

Everything was wrong.

From her hospital bed, she watched with growing surprise as a woman spit water back into a glass and then took it over to the small sink where the faucet sucked it back up.

A flaw in time.

She lay awake at night plotting her escape from the hospital in anticipation of being found by those who wished to harm her, whoever they were.

The wind blew through the thin blanket she'd wrapped around her shoulders. It was early in the morning, she'd brought her passport because of a hunch that it would be important for something she'd have to do, and a few items of clothing. These things were in the blue plastic liner from the trashcan in her hospital room, and she was wearing a pair of too-big shoes she'd found in the closet.

She headed for the tall buildings on the horizon, walking along freeways and through train tunnels. At a crossing surrounded by office buildings, a traffic signal changed and people were set in motion. Their pinched faces as they bumped into her had something cruel about them, as though they were holding a password, a code that would unleash terrible violence on her.

She ate bread crusts and cold French fries out of discarded Styrofoam boxes. Why were they lying about her at the hospital? Why did her body twitch when she saw the uniformed guards posted at the entrances of shops and banks? What had happened to her?

It often felt like she was being annihilated, as though all that was left of her was a lingering sense of despair outside on the curb. She spent her nights huddled on sidewalks, in the waning flicker of broken halogen lights, and it was only after a week or so of this that she realized she hadn't slept since waking up at the hospital at least a month before.

Her existence was an unrelenting stream of impressions. From the city birds, she learned to eat from outdoor patio tables instead of the trash. Old and young men tried to get her into their cars. Once a man tried to pull her into a public toilet, but she kicked him and fled.

One night she was devouring whatever was left on the plates in an outdoor seating area, it must have been late August, a mild night, the patio half deserted but full of wrought-iron furniture and branded umbrellas. A couple on vacation was talking about the food, and she realized it was the first time she could understand what other people were saying; the sounds gained traction on a surface inside her. It was as though she began and ended in the same breath. The man laughed and his teeth showed, large and with food stuck in them.

In the language the couple was speaking, other people had once said to her that she didn't belong, that the language was not hers. A feeling of being turned outside in.

She was having difficulty breathing.

The voices of the vacationing couple carried a premonition of death.

She was Swedish. She was Swedish by not being Swedish.

She hitchhiked north. Learned to say "Sweden." Hiked across the fume-colored grass at the edge of the road. She found that she could sleep when in motion, curled up in the back seats of cars or sitting with her forehead against the dashboard.

In dreams, remnants of some incomprehensible experience searched for corresponding images. She remembered hands in blue latex gloves searching her mouth. A young black man watching her, saying her pain was being recorded. Once she woke up because the car she was in had stopped in traffic. Tall fences and uniformed men. Her body started shuddering so intensely that the woman giving her a lift thought she was having a seizure.

She crossed borders.

She wandered into fields to pee and spied cities in the night, lighting up the sky like grass fires beyond the horizon.

She stole a map at a gas station and seemed to recognize the name *Gothenburg*.

North.

A woman shouted from a balcony, the name she was calling echoed between the tall buildings. I'd bought a bag of bread at the grocery store and was tossing crumbs to the pigeons. A fight had broken out the night before. A group of kids set fire to a car and then threw rocks at the fire trucks and police; the stillness that now lay over the Rabbit Yard was oppressive and restless. As if an evacuation was underway. An older man in a fluttering white jallabia passed by on his way to the same basement where I was going to pray my nighttime prayers. The man recognized me from my visits over the years, nodded, and wished me peace. One hand on his heart.

A corrugated copper building towered over the structures that ringed in the square, its windows shimmering in the violet-gray night. Social and health services. The place the girl from Tundra had called Building T in her account. The place where she thought she'd died, in her world's future.

She had crossed this square, sometimes with Amin. She'd written to me that it was like walking over her own grave.

We were moving to Toronto in the spring, finally, and as I scattered the last of the crumbs from the bag, I realized I'd come here to say goodbye. I wanted to say goodbye to the buildings, chain-link fences, electrical boxes, and cement slabs. Goodbye to what these things still retained of the person I had once been.

Almost fifteen years before I'd stood on this square holding a moving box. It was shortly after I started university, I was on my way to my first apartment, which was a few stops closer to the city. I'd stopped and just stood there. Like now, I'd wanted to keep everything with me. I still remember that night so well. A group of old friends were smoking outside the grocery store and one of them raised a hand in greeting, already half a world away, the chain hanging over his warm-up jacket glimmered like light through the gap of a closed door. Ten years later, he would travel to Syria and die. I took the bus, the box on my lap. I sat down in my new apartment and started writing.

The girl had claimed my books were full of fear. That fear made them beautiful. Maybe it was true. But I'd always thought that most of all they expressed sorrow for the passage of time, a sorrow over how nothing will last.

I thought about my books, about my childhood, about friends who had died, about my parents' fate, and knew that my writing stemmed from what I'd left behind.

I knew the book I was writing now came from Sweden.

Again, the voice shouted from the balcony high above me. It sounded like Mom's voice, which had so often echoed over the square.

Calling me home.

She reached the Öresund Bridge. Crossed parking lots and walked alongside traffic jams. She waited for someone to wave her down and bring her to the other side. The wind splashed her face with sea water. She was impatient, fearing an evil force was about to catch up to her, and finally boarded a train, even though she had no money. She watched the bridge trusses dissolve in speed—the horizon's granitic hues. The first Swedish words she said were, "I don't have a ticket."

She was kicked off but hitchhiked up the coast to Gothenburg's yellow broadleaf trees, which made her remember a man who'd said he liked the fall—a slim man who might have been her real dad.

She spent her nights at a McDonald's, sitting on the uncomfortable plastic furniture. The memories of al-Mima must have been inside her, buried beneath amnesia: waterboarding, strange experiments in which her consciousness was manipulated with electricity and sensory deprivation.

She slept on streetcars and buses, moving away from that which was unnamed but constantly flickering on the outskirts of her memory.

The black line toward Bergsjön, her forehead resting

against a foggy, night-chilled window; she yawned and looked out at the footbridges dripping with rain. She'd been dreaming of a man walking through a mall with a sword slung over his shoulder—so random—she laughed, but noticed tears in her eyes.

She collected empty cans, recycled them, and paid to use the internet at 7-Eleven. Googled the name in the passport. She read about the girl from Belgium, about her fate, which seemed both wrong and eerily familiar.

Why were they lying about her?

Outside the Nordstan shopping mall, groups of girls were wearing headphones with small beads threaded onto the wires and clothing that looked old-fashioned somehow, like it belonged to their parents. She never spoke to them. But sometimes an adult would buy food for her after seeing her sneak leftovers off the sticky plastic trays at McDonald's. Sometimes she ate and sometimes she just sat there, staring at the food they offered her, convinced it was poisoned, or irradiated.

Was she Swedish?

Was she one of them?

Sometimes a name skirted the edge of her mind, and she wondered who that person had been: Liat.

The 52 bus turned off the freeway and stopped on a hill. She woke up to a view of a junkyard, hubcaps and old computer shells in a jumble, and she thought she remembered a similar landscape, an entire world made of ruins and abandoned things, and she felt simultaneously that everything belonged to her and was also withdrawing. She pushed a button on a toilet at the Central Station and the whole world was torn up by questions. Where do I come from? Why is it still here? Why is everything? Existence was like being chained to a clumsy doppelgänger.

She shouldn't exist.

Everything was wrong.

She dreamed of a woman by the sea. The bus stopped, she woke up slowly—the light from a lotus flower on a restaurant sign dulled by rain was hanging in the distance, under colorless skies.

Amin was sitting on the 9 toward Angered in early winter, looking out at the construction sites and furniture warehouses.

She thought his buzz cut made him look like an inmate. Jaw clenched in the drizzly light. She knew his name was Amin and they belonged together and when he got off the streetcar she followed him.

Followed him between tall apartment buildings, their blue paint peeling, a few steps behind, hands shoved in the pockets of a hoodie she'd found at McDonald's. She rushed over and caught the elevator door before it glided shut behind him.

He was leaning against the elevator's rattling wall. Finally, a clue about the person she once had been. Rainwater pooled around his shoes—she remembered his running shoes with the neon-yellow stripe and air cushions. She remembered his patchy black beard-fluff and acne scars. His brown eyes, flecked with gray and green.

He seemed to be emanating a kind of restrained power, like a hot metal wire.

Why did she recognize him and why did he not recognize her?

A moth crept over the graffitied elevator mirror.

He took out a cellphone, typed something, put it back in his jacket. He was getting off on five and she realized that she hadn't pressed a button yet and pressed four. The elevator pinged and stopped. When she didn't get off he turned to her.

"It's a Muslim." Those were his first words to her, and then he stood there, lips parted in a dopey smirk, and when she said, "Huh?" he nodded toward the yellow warning decal showing a trashcan stuck in an elevator doorway and a man being crushed against the ceiling.

"That dude being crushed. He's Muslim," he said, and when she still offered no reaction, he added, "or maybe you know a lot of suedis who are garbagemen?" He laughed, like he was surprised by her stubborn silence. She remembered something. Not him, but someone else, each on their own swing, laughing. Was it childhood? Liat—that name again. Sorrow, dense as scar tissue. What happened to her? She had to know.

Amin reached out and wiped a tear from her cheek, an unexpected, tender gesture that must have meant something to her. She said, "Your name is Amin."

She came to on the back of the moped, the wind hitting her face like air through an open vent, her arms around his slim, tight waist.

Spring days in a whirlwind of illness, barely a year before the attack.

She was living with him. According to her, their relationship was platonic then, sibling-like and close. Amin had a record of drug possession and misdemeanor assault. He was eighteen and had just gotten his own apartment. Rarely saw his mother, never saw his dad. What could he have seen in a seventeen-year-old girl, all on her own, who was clearly unstable? What got him to let her use his shower and sleep on his sofa that first night, after the encounter in the elevator? Why did he welcome her into his life?

Maybe the explanation lay in his relationship to his little sister, who'd been dead for so long, Nour, or in the story about the relationship, which had come to him in part after his childhood—a whisper of a more innocent time, when Dad was at home and Mom was happy.

In the months since she'd arrived in Gothenburg, the girl had scraped together a story about herself that went like this: She had been locked up in a camp somewhere in Sweden, maybe because she was Muslim, which certain memories led her to believe she was. Her true identity had been hidden from her by the Swedish authorities and she was sent to Belgium where they'd tried to trick her into thinking she was someone else, as part of some plan she didn't really understand.

She talked with Amin about this, quite often, and he added his own speculation, like maybe she'd freaked out on hash and taken herself to Brussels. But that whole thing about the couple pretending she was their daughter, that was hella shady.

He smelled of cigarettes and sweat and a cologne he said his cousin bought in the mosque, even though he'd never been there himself. They shared intimate moments while looking out over the streetcar tracks from a footbridge, and he said she could be his sister returned, and maybe that was why she recognized him—and she almost believed him.

He taught her to recognize undercover police cars—pointing them out when they passed by: Volvos with extra sideview mirrors and cameras fixed to the dashboards.

They watched bad movies or chatted about nothing late

into the night and she knew, in an intense and clear way, that he would lead her to the answer to the question about her identity, because they had known each other in her old life. She was so sure that they ended up fighting about it—why didn't he just tell the truth about who they were?

One day he stopped his moped and pointed at a parked bus and it took her a while to see what it was he was trying to point out: the driver was on a break, praying on a mat he'd rolled out in front of the radiator grill, an African man wearing a crocheted cap. Amin stared at him incredulously, spit on the asphalt, and said, "I hate them."

The bus driver bowed, put his forehead to the mat. Traffic roared past.

"Bus drivers?"

"Wallah you're so out of it sometimes. Muslims," Amin said. "I mean those Muslims who keep their heads down and their nose to the grindstone and think that makes them better than other people." He glared at the man. "They think they're better than us, you know what I'm sayin'?"

"Yeah," she said, even though she didn't know—something private and wounded in him was speaking—maybe he was talking about his dad, who she knew had left a long time ago.

"Fucking straight up slave," he said of the praying bus driver, and repeated himself in a way that sounded like a complaint but also like he couldn't believe the man's miserable existence, "fucking slave."

He could spend an hour, unreachable, staring at cigarette butts overflowing from a soda can, then start laughing and drag her out to play shooter games in the arcade at Liseberg, and as they mowed down dinosaurs or zombies with plastic guns, he'd say he was going to move in with his dad in

Norway, or become an airplane mechanic, or go live with a cousin in Germany who had a car dealership.

They traveled between Gothenburg's neighborhoods with a bag full of hash and weed and pills, and ran into guys in windbreakers who shook his hand and mumbled greetings, exchanged rumors—black-haired, unloved boys like himself, shadows on the square, "And what about Zaid, he still in juvie?"

Under the image of the grill's pink-and-blue neon sign in the mirror, Hamad was grim and soldier-like with his full beard and combat pants tucked into high-tops.

That afternoon, the girl and Amin were each eating a mixed grill plate. Later, the three of them would say this encounter was *qadr,* fate, but when it happened it wasn't like that: Amin was trying to avoid being seen—he'd pulled up his hood and kept his eyes fixed on the greasy plastic tabletop.

Hamad sounded disappointed when he said hello, he even put on a plaintive and, she thought, fake pious tone, "Where do you say your Friday prayers, brother?"

Amin lied and said he worked Fridays and then they spent a while talking about people they both knew. Hamad had a gritty, awful heft about him, but she thought something magnetic too, as she poked at her food, listening; the man behind the counter shouted, "Wrap with extra everything," and even though Hamad's order was up, his gaze bore into Amin a little longer.

Out on the square a moped buzzed past carrying three children, barely older than ten. One girl in front, her sparkly purple veil rippling in the wind, two boys on the back. Their shouts faded and left behind a feeling she couldn't articulate. Something about being a girl in Sweden. Memories she couldn't access.

Hamad wished them peace and disappeared across the square with his food.

When it happened between her and Amin she knew it was her first time ever. Amin sat on the edge of the bed afterward and she took in his naked back, the bend of his neck, the light spilling in from outside turning his downy hair a luminous blue. Feeling how the world around her had aged. How a mark was made. Her first time.

My first time, Liat.

Amin got up, opened a window, lit a joint; she laid there and tried to keep the memories surfacing because of his nighttime silhouette at bay. Couldn't.

"Why should anyone have to see their dad getting stripped?" she asked.

"Maybe he was in the hospital?"

"It was, like, guards undressing him."

The things she remembered must have shocked Amin sometimes. But maybe that was part of what he liked about her—he didn't really know who he was either.

Maybe he put his mouth to the crack in the window and exhaled the smoke.

"In fourth grade," he said, "you had to have Air Force Ones."

"What are Air Force Ones?"

"Sneakers. Everyone in my class had them but me."

She lay on her side, hands under the pillow. Right now was good. She thought Amin had something vulnerable and remarkable about him, and she wished she could stretch the moment out, make it last longer.

"This fool Mahmoud was on me about it every day. He was, like, a head taller than everyone else in our grade. He was all: 'Ugly shoes.' Every day. 'Ugly shoes.' Getting the whole class to laugh at me, you know what I'm sayin'?"

"Yes," she said.

"So I kept bugging Mom, and eventually she bought me a pair. It musta cost her a month of groceries." He laughed, short and bitter. Pinching the joint to get the last hit. The image of her dad was still in her mind. He was naked in a room and someone was forcing him to bend over. She squeezed her eyes tight, then looked at Amin again.

"What happened?" she asked. "Did he stop teasing you? The guy?"

"Mahmoud. Did he stop teasing me? Nah. You know what he did?"

"What did he do?"

"He saw me lacing up my Air Force Ones. During the first recess. He stood there, just staring at them for a long time. I thought he was jealous, you know what I'm sayin', because his were like a year old and mine were box fresh. But then he busted out laughing, and he said it again. 'Ugly shoes.'"

She didn't really get it. Amin's rage had returned, a hard tension that frightened her a little.

"Were they the wrong shoes?"

"They were the same shoes as everybody else's," he said. "But it didn't matter. That was the point, Nour. Do you know why he was laughing?"

"No?"

"The whole time he'd been waiting for me to buy the same shoes as him. So he could show me just how much power he had—he could still get the whole schoolyard to laugh at my shoes."

His posture was slightly bent, a few vertebrae in his neck sticking out. The cherry of the joint singed his fingertips and he swore softly, changed hands, and blew on them. "You gotta understand. People like us, we have no power," he said. "Your dad had no power. That's why they stripped him in front of you. To show you."

She didn't know what to say. Emptiness streamed through her, an icy chill.

"Your nose is bleeding again," Amin said. She wiped it with her finger and licked the finger clean, a worthless little gesture that felt new.

She wasn't sure why she'd slept with him. She'd made the first move, maybe because of the power she felt when they were together, that buzzing behind her forehead.

Interwoven.

"Who was that at the grill?"

"Who?" Amin said. One of the things she liked about him was that he was so bad at lying. She mocked him, exaggerating his tone:

"Who?"

He finished smoking, sat down with her. It was the first time she'd been kissed there, between her shoulder blades. He didn't want to talk about it. She said his name, a question, and he answered:

"Hamad."

"Hamad who?"

"He used to be me," he mumbled, his lips on the nape of her neck.

"Be you?" she asked. That's when he stopped kissing her.

"He had my block, my clients. Then he bounced to Syria

last winter. I took over his burner and everything."

"Syria?" she said, because she didn't know much about the war then.

He made finger guns and shook them, like rat-tat-tat-tat, but soundless.

"Daesh," he said. "He came back two months ago. Yani, terrorist."

She touched the bulletproof glass, as though she were reaching for something in the sky. No orderlies or doctors were with us in the room, but the camera in the corner was on and I assumed her doctor would watch the video later.

"I knew I had to be near them. Amin and Hamad," she said. "They were spectacular. Like Oh Nana Yurg," she added, chuckling at the thought. When she turned to face me, I could tell by her expression and posture that she was gone—the other part of her consciousness had appeared and was now inhabiting her body. She said something in a soft but unmelodious language. Flemish. I later asked a Belgian author to listen to it and translate:

"*Where's my family? Why have you locked me up here?*"

She'd stopped giving me pages—as far as I knew her story about the future was over. She had died in that bed, and her consciousness had been recorded or saved by a machine, which had sent her into Annika Isagel's body, in another world and another time… Per the logic of her story.

She searched her surroundings anxiously, eyes roving the clinic's walls, the fence outside the window, the landscape beyond it, and then after a few breaths, she was back, as suddenly as she'd disappeared. She picked at a flake of paint on the window frame.

"Will you touch my cheek?" she asked.

I stayed in my chair, imagining this cruelty would safeguard my innocence here, in Tundra's visitors' room. When she noticed I wasn't going to she said, "When are you moving?"

"In winter."

"So you've actually made a decision now?" I nodded. "Does it feel strange to be leaving your country?"

"I don't know if this has ever been my country," I said.

The sun brightened and for a few seconds the grease and dirt on the bulletproof glass stood out as clearly as white paint—continents on a fading map.

"You know the essay my dad wrote after Mom died?"

"The one nobody wanted to publish?"

"Yeah. He wrote that what happened to us was the same as what happened to the Jews, and to the Armenians. The Bosnians. He wrote a long list of people who had been annihilated, because he didn't think the Swedes understood what they were doing." She seemed to have given this a lot of thought, her voice was composed, full of reason. "But they weren't afraid of that history like we were. I know that now. We read about genocide and stuff in school, but it was all about how sad it was for everyone who'd been subjected to it, not what happened to those who did the killing, how they'd destroyed their words, and everything that gave life meaning. We learned nothing about the emptiness." Her eyes narrowed, she sighed and said, "There's so much I could tell you. To prove I come from the future. If you'd only believe me. That's why I started writing to you." A passing cloud tempered the light, which flickered across her face. "So you would believe me."

One early summer day in the 1950s a woman turned up at an airport near Tokyo with a passport issued by a nation that did not exist. When the customs officer pointed it out, the woman asked for an atlas, opened it to Europe, and ran her finger along the border between Spain and France. She claimed that her homeland was near Andorra and became more and more upset when she couldn't find it. Her passport was well-used and had stamps from a number of airports; she spoke several languages and had various European currencies in her wallet. The police were called. Because she'd become hysterical over the—apparent—disappearance of her homeland, they locked her in a room at the airport and searched her possessions.

When the door was opened about an hour later, the woman was gone. She had left no trace.

Incidents like this occur a couple of times a decade. People going into convincing detail about countries that don't exist. Every time I read one of these stories I thought of the incredible loneliness in not being able to share your world with a single other person.

Isra and I sorted our belongings into boxes: what was coming with us and what would be left behind. It was slow going, maybe because it was a labor of grief. On certain nights, as I sat going through my books and notes, or just a box of clothes, I felt like I was searching a ruin, sifting through the remnants of the life I thought I was going to live, but that had now ceased to exist.

I wrote about the girl at the clinic from time to time, searching for a beginning, an opening image. I went through my notes again and again, dogged by the thought of having missed something important.

I revisited the leaked material from al-Mima. Thousands of hours of torture recorded on cellphones and video cameras.

There was reason to suspect that the black boxes or closets the witnesses had described as "computers" were some kind of neurological recording apparatus, or even quantum computers, for which K5GS had a number of patents, remarkably enough—in theory, calculators connected to an endless number of similar structures in parallel worlds. An endless number of memories. I looked through the films showing people drowning, crying, and shuddering on cold cement floors. A library of screams out in the desert's light. I wondered if the person who the girl at Tundra thought she was wasn't just a feedback wave that had flowed into Annika Isagel's brain after it had been connected to al-Mima's black boxes. A sort of static or spillage.

A dream from the desert.

I sat with my sleeping daughter so I could listen to her breathe.

She laughed in her sleep. I touched her forehead. If she disappeared, I would too.

Why couldn't I forget the girl at Tundra? It was no surprise that she was writing, her illness itself was like writing. I felt isolated from my time and my country; I heard my daughter breathing in the dark and a wall inside me was about to collapse.

Maybe it all had to do with our move. Soon we would be leaving Sweden and these stories behind.

Hamad's dad covered his flowerbeds with decaying leaves to protect them from night frost.

"This will all be sunflowers," he said. "In the summer." He pulled off his tattered gardening gloves and held them in one hand. The dome of sky above the suburban houses was cornflower blue and as smooth as velvet. He was short and slender-limbed but still had something authoritative about him. His padded jacket made me think of hunting or riding.

"This life was never enough for Hamad." He looked around the garden. "This Swedish life was never enough."

Beyond the brick roofs and chimneys shined the windows of Hasselbo where Amin had lived, and where he and the girl at Tundra had tooled around on his moped before Hamad got his claws into them.

"Even as a child he was always asking about Syria, about his cousins. He thought there was something better for him there. He thought that's where he came from."

Amin's mother was in some sort of contact with Hamad's family, and had apparently given them a positive impression of our meeting. This was how my visit at Hamad's childhood home had come to pass. It was difficult for the dad to get close to the subject—he poked around in his flowerbeds, telling me about his own life, about studying economics while working as a janitor at night and how his wife was a specialist nurse at a private clinic, about them buying this house seventeen years ago and the comprehensive renovations he'd carried out. Only then did he mention his dead son. The mastermind of the attack on Hondo's. His head was bare and still hot from having worked in the garden, steam rose around his shaved scalp.

"Why do you think he went back?"

"Aren't you Muslim?" More than anything, he sounded contemplative. "Doesn't the Koran say we're supposed to make war on the infidels? Kill them?"

There was a theological argument against what he was saying: the verses regarded a specific historical situation, and were mitigated and restricted by other parts of the Koran. But that's not what he was after. As far as I understood, he was

Muslim himself, but not particularly devout.

"He broke his mother's heart when he left," he said. "Mine too, but she's Alevi. Do you know what that means?" I nodded—one of the minorities persecuted by Daesh in Syria.

A streetcar glided past, heading toward the apartment blocks.

"Did you ever meet Amin or his wife?"

"We didn't even know Hamad was back in Sweden," he said. Then Hamad's mother opened the front door and called me into the warmth. He stayed outside, in the cold.

We sat across from each other in leather armchairs. On the glass table between us she'd set out a metal tray with a pot of tea, cups, and cookies. We'd only been in touch by email and I wasn't sure how to begin the conversation. She noticed me looking at a carpet under the table. It had an intricate geometrical pattern in red and black and might have been the only thing in the room that didn't suggest Swedish upper middle class.

"Nomads in the mountains weaved it on a loom, which they dismantled each time they moved," she said. "Hence the irregularities." She pointed out a few lines that weren't entirely symmetrical. "We brought it with us from Damascus, from our apartment."

She poured us both some tea, and the way she held her cup made her look as if she were freezing and craved the heat.

"Are you writing about her? The girl who shot Amin?"

"About the events of that night."

"And why not?" She was wearing a black turtleneck and an elaborate necklace from a Scandinavian silversmith—I would have guessed it was very expensive and by some prominent artist or designer.

She was still holding the hot cup, and the spoon clinked against the porcelain—her hands were shaking.

"How is she?"

"She's locked in a mental institution. She's very…sick. She suffering from schizophrenia."

The elder of Hamad's two younger siblings came into the hall carrying a green gym bag, and her mom reminded her to bring home her team uniform so that it could go in the laundry. The daughter told her to stop nagging—resplendent bickering about the practicalities that hold the days and nights together. I stirred a spoonful of honey into my tea, waiting for Hamad's mother to return to our conversation, but it seemed to take her a while to remember I was even in the room. She kept looking into the empty hall and her face was no more than a surface, abandoned and eerie—then she was back, smiling apologetically at me.

"I'm sorry," she said.

"No problem."

"Maybe all refugees are crazy." Her laughter was joyless. "Because we've lost the world that gave us meaning." Finally she took another sip of tea and put the cup down, casting a knowing glance at the front door her daughter had just shut behind her. "She's trying to hide it, but I can see she's inherited it from us. The fear." She studied my face. "You have it in you, too, don't you? From your parents?"

"Maybe," I replied, and thought about the moving boxes at home, the airplane tickets we'd recently bought, forever being chased by worry.

Something in her way of speaking reminded me of my own mother and others of her generation—people who thought they could come here and become Swedish, unlike us, their children.

"Hamad was always good in school, write that," she said firmly. "And write that even after he started having problems with the police, he could have become a doctor with his grades. He was studying at the university right up until he went to Syria. Biology, chemistry. Online classes. But nobody knew, of course."

Each time she fell silent and we were left looking at each other across the glass table, the large house felt desolate, as though it had been abandoned long ago, and then, each time, she would offer that polite, apologetic smile. I took it as an attempt to restore dignity, which was futile considering my errand.

"There's a video," she said. She cleared her throat and ran her hand down the crease of her pants. "They say it's him. Killing those people in Syria."

"I've seen it."

"I watch it at night. When my husband is asleep." Silence swallowed the house again. I could hear us breathing. With a short nod, in an intimate tone she said: "I watch it every night. All you can see is the eyes through the mask. I'm trying to tell if it's really him."

I was reminded of something Isra once said, about those who left their families for the war. They would drown in their mothers' tears.

"At one point, he wanted to change his name. Did you know that? Have the newspapers written about that?" Helpless rage somewhere inside her. I shook my head. She smoothed the pleat in her trousers again. "Maybe it was in fourth or fifth grade. What was it that he wanted to be called? Harry? Larry?"

She saw only a fragment of Hamad's face. It was hanging in the small mirror, vibrating along with the motor.

"Our dead look like they're sleeping," he said. The car was running even though they had been parked for almost ten minutes. Because he wanted to be able to escape, thought the girl, who by then even thought of herself as Nour sometimes.

Amin sat in the passenger seat next to Hamad, pretending to listen. Mostly Amin thought Hamad was a nag, he would later confide in her. Overkill.

"They're birds now. Birds in paradise," Hamad said. They had been to Friday prayer in an apartment in Hasselbo. Hamad didn't like regular mosques. Everybody who went to one was a hypocrite or a pretender. Yani fake Muslims. She prayed in the women's area, which was just a closet where someone had pushed the clothing to one side and laid out a prayer mat.

A moth crawled over the cracked vinyl backseat. By now she knew she was the only one who could see the moths. She'd talked to Amin about it, but all he did was shrug.

Hamad said, "This photographer. A Russian. He noticed it." Again he went still, mouth half open. *Ping. Ping.* Pigeons hopped around a broken wastebasket, tearing at cigarette butts and silvery candy wrappers in the afternoon light. The pinging meant fasten your seatbelt. "He said…Assad's dead look like they're screaming…" That's how Hamad talked, in bursts, punctuated by reflective silences that didn't seem like they should be interrupted. *Ping.* "Their faces are straight up purple, tongues sticking out and shit… *Astaghfirullah.*" The last part was a prayer of forgiveness for having used the word "shit." *Ping. Ping.* His face in the juddering mirror—she thought it was like he came from a denser universe.

"He said. Yani, the photographer. He said. Your dead. Brother. They look like they're sleeping." He scratched the tip of his nose, gestured with his hand. "He noticed. The difference between their dead and ours." He shut off the motor, finally, and the flutter of pigeon wings could be heard; she thought it sounded like bare feet running down stairs.

That same weekend. Amin had parked his 180 by the on-ramp of the Älvsborg Bridge where they had a view of the harbor. One of the best places to share a joint. Sometimes she smoked too. A couple lost weeks between worlds.

She and Amin on a moped, the first hint of fall in the air, in the fog around the cranes and trucks, the thing about the dead had stuck with her. How Hamad said it. *Our dead.*

Memories of the woman she thought was her mother grew clearer and clearer, the one who'd been murdered or maybe run over. She took a drag and passed the joint to Amin. Welding sparks blinked down in the harbor, the feeble light of falling stars. She knew she wanted to be in a world with her own dead. Share death with someone.

She used Amin's phone to make a call that very night. Hamad's voice was rough and sleepy, and she told him how they'd killed her mother. She heard him take a few breaths. She waited for him to speak, but he just listened.

"They did something to the Muslims where I lived," she said. "They killed us."

"The Swedes did?"

She moved out of Amin's apartment in the beginning of October, because Hamad told her she couldn't stay there as long as she and Amin were unmarried. She listened to him because his talk about war and death made an impression, resonating with a thick darkness inside her, and because, like Amin, he glowed with meaning—both promising and threatening.

She lived with a woman Hamad connected her with. They studied Islam together a couple of times a week—a group of women meeting in an apartment in Hasselbo, reading from the Koran and talking about the Holy War to restore the caliphate. They never went to regular mosques and they didn't answer the greetings of other Muslims. When Hamad visited, he'd speak to them from behind a hanging sheet. She sensed that she was fulfilling her destiny. More and more often, she saw moths, which she associated with a mission, still unknown—something with Amin and Hamad—they crawled over the walls in the room where she slept and swarmed around streetlights when she walked between the buildings. She was full of buzzing, unknown powers. She couldn't tell if she was very happy or deeply sad.

She was an exciting feature of the sisters' meetings. They kept asking her to tell them what she remembered from the camp where she'd seen guards abuse people and where Muslims were forced to eat pork. A few times she made up details when she couldn't actually remember. She was a survivor and a clear sign of the infidels' untrustworthiness. It made her feel chosen in way that must have spoken to her illness, to the schizophrenia at work inside her, and to her conviction that something important lay ahead. She watched leaves fall over courtyards and playgrounds, thinking God knew about each and every one of them, and God was guiding her, but really it was neither religion nor ideology that had drawn her to Hamad and his circle, it was an internal wound that whispered about a vague but incredible wrong to be avenged.

She missed Amin less than she'd expected to, but sometimes she did think about his moods, the snide comments that would have peppered the grandest of Hamad's expositions, which he shared with the sisters from his spot behind the sheet. She knew the three of them—she, Hamad, and Amin—were meant to be close, and she told the sisters about Amin, saying he was a nice person who had taken care of her. But the sisters said that men could not control their urges, and the way they laughed reminded her of other women who'd laughed in the same way, hands over their mouths.

She didn't think as often about all she did not remember, all she didn't know about herself. Who she was. Why she'd been in a hospital in Brussels.

From behind the sheet, Hamad said that many warriors in Syria were in need of wives, and it was a woman's duty to support them. He talked about the black widows in Russia who had blown themselves up in Moscow's subway or taken hostages in theaters and schools to avenge their murdered relatives in Chechnya. She sat in the spartan apartment where they normally gathered, where no one actually seemed to live, and listened with devotion. On some days she didn't think exploding into pieces would be strange at all.

During one of his visits, Hamad called on her so they could speak about Amin.

A man on the other side of a washed-out piece of fabric was telling her the time had finally come to get married.

The wedding. The simplest possible. Held in Hamad's apartment, where he was a subletter. She sat with her sisters in Hamad's son's room, but for some unknown reason the boy was not there—the truth, later revealed by the media, was that before his trip to the crumbling terrorist state in Syria, Hamad had lost custody of his son after beating the boy and his mother.

They sat on the floor, as usual, and the sisters were ceremonious, tense, happy, jealous. Some were dressed up in bright, silky dresses, the embroidery and beads making them look like princesses. Hamad regarded them with contempt. She had been lent a simple dress by one of the women she lived with. She brought a teddy bear with her that was leaking small bits of foam from a tear. She lined them up in a row on the floor. Amin, Hamad, and a couple of other men whose voices she didn't recognize were talking in the living room—she could hear their raucous laughter through the door.

She hadn't seen Amin since she'd moved out. Hamad had explained that Amin was on his own journey of spiritual purification and it'd taken longer for him to accept certain truths about life and death.

She realized that maybe, in spite of everything, she longed to see his eyes, which like hers had lost far too much to ever see happiness. Suddenly, she wanted all of the guests to leave. His hands, frightening yet tender. *Congratulations. May God grant you patience.* His lips. People eventually slipping out into the cold, then Amin sticking his head back into the room—serious, secretive—and flashing a cryptic smile.

"Hamad wants to talk to us."

The three of them sat on a plush sectional. Hamad was combing his fingers through his beard. He was dressed like it was any other day, in his black kameez and a pair of sweatpants with a white stripe. She thought, as she so often did when she saw him, of the war, its power that had made him tough and simple, like a thing hewn from rock.

Hands in her lap, she felt the need to take in some of that power in order to keep going.

"Those who go first into the fire curse those who follow," Hamad said before taking a couple of deep breaths and starting to cry, sudden and shaking, but still worthy of respect, yani regal. She looked to Amin for direction, the correct interpretation of this crying warrior, but Amin's face was blank and she couldn't tell if he was moved by Hamad's tears or if it was the most embarrassing thing he'd ever seen.

For a long time, Hamad hid his face in his hands, but then the tears stopped abruptly. He looked up and said, "Those who follow curse those who go before. But God says they will be doubly punished."

She thought he might be talking about what he'd done in Syria, necessary crimes against any human conception of goodness and against a number of God's laws too, possibly, beneath a sky that fell under the supersonic booms of fighter planes. But he was only talking about Amin and himself, it turned out, about hash and pills and the clients Amin had taken over when Hamad had left the country.

"We have a lot of sin on our consciences, brother."

She noticed this all had a practiced quality to it, including the tears. A moth fluttered by her face and she fought the urge to wave it away.

Hamad reached for his laptop, turned it on, and showed them drawings of Muslims: pictures that were intimately familiar in a way that made her hands and legs quake.

Outside the window, darkness had fallen.

She was given the job of making a flag with Daesh's symbol, which was actually a seal the Prophet, peace be upon him, stamped on his letters.

The flag was to be black and have specific dimensions, and because she had a hard time getting ahold of fabric, she bought black trash bags, cut them up, and taped them together with black masking tape. Then she sat with a brush and painted the emblem on the black plastic.

There is no God but God.

Even after all of our conversations I still can't entirely account for why she and Amin participated in the attack on Hondo's. For instance—along with everyone who has tried to make sense of it—I'm still not sure how Amin was radicalized. Acquaintances and family members who have spoken in interviews and police interrogations, as well as in conversations with me, have noted his lack of interest in religion, that he even disliked devout Muslims for their righteousness and meekness. He didn't pray regularly and had drunk alcohol as recently as a couple of weeks before the attack on the comic book store—of course, that could have only been a diversion tactic, to avoid rousing suspicion.

The girl's path, in some sense, is shrouded in darkness, too. She had nightmares about what she would later believe was the Rabbit Yard; stray sequences, often centered around everyday objects—a stretch of chain-link fence, sandwiches, plastic cutlery, a soccer goal—nonetheless saturated with a vast, stifling fear. She didn't just think she was missing a past, but also a future. Even though she didn't drink, she sometimes smoked hash, even after she married Amin. Other times though, she seemed completely consumed by her (possibly superficial) piety.

Maybe it was as simple but as complex as this: Hamad offered her and Amin a dream that accommodated them. So she sat down and wrote the word "God" on a flag made of trash bags.

They face each other. Their chests are heaving, fast. Amin's sweat gives his curls an oily sheen.

After a period of silence, the megaphone starts blaring again, out there among the police cars and the people.

"You have to let him go, Amin," she says, but another sharp wedge of pain drives itself between her eyes and she stumbles backward, steadying herself on a bookcase.

Everything is inside her, everything that happens to her in the future, everything these events will lead to: the citizen contract, the Crusading Hearts surrounding her and Liat in the snow, the video playing at the bus stops, the storm blowing in over Sweden.

"It's too late," Amin says. "It's too late."

"I had a best friend," she says. "Liat. She was named Liat. We used to sit in the swings."

Amin wets his lips. "Liat. What kind of name is that?" His eyes flit. By now, he's only holding on to a few hairs on Göran Loberg's head.

She says the name again, *Liat*, mostly to herself, to taste its sound and experience the swell of emotion it brings up.

"We used to watch a video of you." She holds her cellphone

out. "Liat and I used to watch this video all the time."

"You watched the video you just recorded?"

She nods.

"Yes, this video."

"What are you talking about?" Amin asks, and then repeats himself, hysterically, again and again: "What are you talking about, what are you talking about, what are you talking about?"

"I came here from the future, Amin. Listen, please. What we've planned to do here tonight will lead to emptiness."

His body is limp.

"What fucking emptiness?"

"They'll put us in camps. Normal Muslims. If we kill these people, Muslims won't be able to live here anymore."

Amin doesn't reply. Time swells again, the moment becomes a booming focal point. Loberg's crumpled at Amin's feet, the duct tape over his mouth reflecting the blue light from outside.

Everything is inside her. The metal box with Mom's ashes. The plague that killed so many in the Rabbit Yard. Building T. Bilal screaming as he clings to the toilet.

Eventually, Amin says, "Good." Just the one word. And she understands. She understands why he's here. He thinks it's good this will lead to the bus driver they once saw not being able to live here anymore—praying his prayers during his break—and everybody else who keeps their heads down and thinks they're better than Amin. It'll be good for them to see that this is war and they have to choose sides, like he has—or die, which soon he will too. He gets a good grip on Loberg's hair and yanks him up.

Everything moves slowly.

The blue lights slide across the walls, slow as a tide—her

hand finds the machine gun's grip, and without actually thinking about what she's doing, *Amin*—

"Amin!" She shouts his name as she squeezes the trigger, shouts to warn him.

"Amin!"

She squeezes the trigger once but fires three shots—it happens automatically—the weapon nearly flies out of her hands.

Amin.

He falls backward into the flag. It comes loose and sinks down over him like a wide black wing.

Everything could have been different.

Amin.

She squats at his side, digs him out of the black plastic.

Two shots hit him, one in the shoulder above the vest, one in the throat.

"Who's shooting? Hello in there! Who's shooting?" The voices from the street.

Amin, your delicate lips. Your long eyelashes. Her hands tremble as she peels the black flag from his face. He coughs and blood sprays his chin.

She says, "Amin." The name that has pursued her, and she takes his hand, which is limp as though with sleep. He lifts his head and nestles into her.

She has saved them.

Nothing has to happen now.

She props him in a half-seated position against the bookshelf and tries to wipe his chin with the flag, but the black plastic only smears the blood around. Amin is pale; he coughs, curt and bubbling, and says the name of his long-dead sister. He smiles like he's just woken up.

Interwoven.

Balagan.

One of the police vans outside turns on its headlights, brightness fills the store, and everything is sharp and clear: Amin's closed eyes and open mouth, the coins and bills in the blood, the victims' cuffed bodies here and there, the disarray of comics and books, the cash register Hamad kicked off the counter, his body by the window—it all looks sort of discarded and worthless, as if the white light through the window is illuminating more than the objects, but life and time itself in a final state of waste.

She gets to her feet and hurries over to the window. The SWAT team is by the door.

Think.

She curls up behind some boxes and feels a stinging loneliness, a whirling, the impossibility of holding on to a single thought. Think think. Top five crazy things about having traveled through time. Number five: Could she find herself as a child? Four. Think think think. She picks up Amin's knife and cuts the zip ties that locked the man in the bomb vest to the door handle. She opens it onto a winter night.

More cameras than she can count.

God God God God.

Journalists and TV cameras, crowds of people all filming with cellphones, the roar of wind and human voices, everything mixed together in the snowy rain—she puts her hands up and screams over all of it:

"I was killed!" Her voice is a hoarse shriek. "I was killed by the Swedish government!" Tears draw icy channels down her cheeks. "It's over," she screams, without entirely knowing what she means. "It's over."

7

Have you ever set out to search
for a missing half?
The piece that isn't shapely, elegant, simple.
The half that's ugly, heavy, abrasive.

—Shailja Patel, *Migritude*

Blue-gray clouds hung over the clinic. Something was making the inmates restless, making them roam the corridors and scream in their locked rooms. The girl and I stood at the window. Even though I would visit Tundra once more, this was, in a way, the last time I was seeing her, and the premonition of this may have made us both reserved.

"They're letting me watch the movie tonight," she said.

"*The Seventeenth of February*?" The film about the events of the previous year had simply used the date as its title. I'd seen it in a movie theater but had avoided the infected debate that followed its premiere.

"The doctors say it might be good for me," she said. She was scratching her hands again, in that vaguely self-harming way. "It might promote healing."

A guard sat next to the camera and fiddled with her cellphone, playing a game or texting. I said it was hard to imagine that seeing the film would be good for her.

"They've changed some things, huh?"

I nodded. We stood near the window and the chill from through the glass was streaming over my skin.

"A number of things. There was a lot of talk about it

in the media."

I wanted to keep discussing the film's interventions in the story, the changes that had troubled me when I'd first seen it, but I noticed the shift in her posture that I'd come to associate with the other part of her taking over, the part that was a Belgian girl who'd been transported to al-Mima and who might be remembering even more of that place.

She tugged at her hijab, tucking a lock of hair under the fabric.

By then I was familiar enough with the change to know it was useless to try and talk to her when she was like this, so I held my tongue and looked out over the rays of light and darkness in the flat September sky. More than fifteen minutes later, she was back. Like always, it took another few minutes before she broke the silence. As though she had to reorient herself in time and space.

"When is your flight leaving?"

"Two weeks."

"How will you bring everything with you? All your stuff?"

"We've packed a container and are shipping it over."

"In two weeks?"

"Yes," I said. I had questions but they wouldn't come out.

Maybe it was the same for her. She nodded to herself. Her eyes grew wet. She said, almost inaudibly, "A love poem."

A fist or a head pounded against a wall one floor down. The noise kept going for a while and by the time she looked up at me she'd disappeared again. I waited for the part of her I was speaking to—and with which I would always be interwoven somehow—to return, but when that didn't happen I said goodbye, even though I knew she didn't understand Swedish. She pulled away when I tried to touch her cheek.

During the bus ride home, the first snow of the year fell, heavy and wet. I wondered whom it was sitting with the doctor in the clinic's TV room. If it was the Belgian girl or the one I'd known, the girl with memories of a world that never was, a future she thought she'd prevented.

In the movie about the events of February seventeenth, she's depicted as an ordinary girl from the ghetto who falls prey to Amin. He manipulates her using religion and the threat of violence. Her Belgian citizenship isn't mentioned, nor is her time at al-Mima. Otherwise, some details are correct—movements and expressions taken straight from the cellphone video.

Amin, in front of the black flag, wearing a sweatband embroidered with Arabic script—an embellishment.

"In the name of the Commander of the Faithful and for every Muslim's honor," he says, but stops himself.

She must be blinking, dazed, at the TV, with a sense of a dual reality.

I looked out the bus window, out into streaming streetlights, out onto small villages nestling together, single-story homes and rows of townhouses clustered around grocery stores and shuttered post offices.

I wonder what kind of answer she'd anticipated when she asked if I felt hopeful about this country.

In the film, Amin kills the artist before the police storm the shop and shoot him. Yet another thing the filmmakers changed. To slit the artist's throat, he doesn't use a box cutter, he uses a utility knife with a crescent-shaped blade—an exquisite detail. As the blood spills out, the actor throws himself backward so it sprays the terrorists' faces.

I once asked her if the future she remembered could be stopped by foiling the attack, didn't that mean the genocide, from one perspective, was justified, or at least caused by Muslims themselves? But what if it's the opposite? If the images in her mind can't be stopped, those pictures from her future, doesn't it imply that there's a force in the world that runs deeper than the superficial events of history? A secret force. An incredible force. A storm.

I wondered if her skin crawled with madness, too, as she watched the scene. The artist's corpse on the floor. The police storming the shop. The girl detonating her bomb vest.

If she'd gone out on the balcony after the movie, maybe a little snow would have been blowing in through the bars meant to keep inmates from jumping, and maybe she cupped her hands into a bowl, as if in prayer, to catch a few snowflakes.

During one of our conversations she told me that it was snowing on the night she'd gone up to the hospital window, because it had snowed in her last memory of the future, which was perhaps the memory of her death. In saying this, I knew she was trying to formulate something she'd always known. Our shadows are stuck to us. Stalk us.

The gravestones looked weighty and dense, like meteorites lodged in the frozen grass. Isra, our daughter, and I were walking to Mom's grave for the last time. Our flight was leaving in two days. I had a bouquet of orange lilies wrapped in plastic and newspaper. We passed Hamad's and Amin's graves without stopping—Amin's grave was marked with a simple metal sign, Hamad's with a glossy black stone engraved with his dates of birth and death. I put the bouquet down beneath high-voltage power lines. Stood a while in silence. A few days prior I'd called Dad and said goodbye to his voicemail.

"The first time I met her, she was crying." Isra was next to me and wrapped in a scarf, our daughter was leaning on her, shivering and bored. "Isn't that strange? She looked up at me and cried."

"You believe her," she said, and let go of our daughter, who ran off to climb the lone chestnut tree growing large among the stones.

"Some of what she wrote might have been true," I said. "Something did take possession of her body when she was at al-Mima. A memory of another world, a possible future. Maybe they weren't trying to implant false memories, but to scan...the future. I don't know, Isra."

"Does that frighten you?"

"What she wrote frightened me."

"But the world is already different from what she thinks she remembers, right?" Isra said.

The wind picked up, it made the tree branches sway around our daughter, who was holding on between the earth and sky. I nodded. Even though parts of the video from Hondo's were shown in the Swedish media during discussions about Islam, and even though new laws had been put in place to regulate the influx of refugees and to counteract "radical Islam"—primarily in the public housing programs in big cities—no laws like what the girl described had been passed. There was no citizen contract; the Rabbit Yard had not become a camp for enemies of the Swedish state.

"She cried," I said. "As though I was someone who could be wanted."

Our daughter waved to us from the chestnut tree, the movement scaring away a couple of cold magpies. I shouted, "Be careful." She'd never be a secure being.

"What do we owe her?" I asked. "The girl from Tundra? Don't we owe her something for what she did?"

Isra rested her head on my shoulder. I loved her for her

courage, for her way of finding the fortune in misfortune, for her wisdom.

"I know the names of the trees here," she said. "Chestnut. Maple. I don't know those words in English or Arabic."

On our way to the bus stop, I stopped at Amin's and Hamad's graves, crouched down, and brushed the dirt from Amin's aluminum plaque. Our daughter asked, "Did you know them?"

There on the ground, I felt the chill running through the world. Whatever I'd say would be a lie. Whatever I'd say would be the truth.

A grenade explodes in a neighborhood nearby, shaking the ground. Hamad has a hard time breathing through the wet balaclava. The gun is heavy, but he's used to heavier things than a Kalashnikov. Five men with their hands tied behind their backs are kneeling in front of him, in that persistent rain: four soldiers, their ranks torn off their olive-green uniform shirts; and one man not in a uniform, a guy in sneakers and civilian clothing whom Hamad has to kill for some unknown reason—the guy is kneeling at the end of the row, face swollen, muddy, and obscured by wet hair. In a troubling way, he seems familiar—he stares at Hamad with a single bloodshot eye, surprised.

The gnawing worry that he's forgotten something.

"Wait," the guy says in Arabic. Hamad recognizes the accent but can't place it. "It's me."

What does he mean, "It's me?" It's hard to make out his features behind that hair. The rain splashes on the walls, gushing and whispering, runs into Hamad's eyes, and the gun is so heavy that what's not supposed to happen happens—the barrel he's pressing to the back of the first prisoner's head wavers a little, back and forth.

He decides to wipe the rain out of his eyes even though it might look bad on video. As if he's wiping away tears.

"I'm you," the prisoner says. Is he laughing? "I'm you." The guy tries to get up but the warrior holding the black flag kicks him in the side so he falls back to his knees.

When you lie behind a wall, aim into the light, fire off a salvo, and a blurry figure fifty meters away collapses into a heap, it's funny, if anything. Nothing has a shine to it afterward, no power rains down on you from heaven. But this—executing a person with their hands tied behind their back—is something else, and it takes a surprising effort. If Hamad were to equate the feeling with something it would be the second when you jump off the ten meter diving board: you've climbed the old diving tower with your buddies and are up there, looking down, yani masculinity test, and one by one they jump and become small white explosions below, and you're the last one, sticking your toes over the edge and leaning into the emptiness.

The gun kicks in his hand. The kneeling man goes limp and falls face down in the clay. Everything is over before Hamad has a chance to register it. He feels like whooping, not for joy but to release what built up inside him as he took aim at the guy. He moves on to the next prisoner and only hesitates for a breath this time. The gunshot is strangely muted, like a New Year's firework. The dead body curls up, a question mark in a puddle of water.

He shoots number three and is, like, zoned out: he's thinking about the film he watched last night on the laptop he brought from Sweden. An action flick he wants to finish after dawn prayer. So what if some of the stricter brothers disapprove of him consuming the *kuffar*'s entertainment. He shoots number four quickly and presses the barrel to the nape of the last prisoner's neck; he's about to pull the trigger when that feeling returns—there's something important he's supposed to remember. It irritates him that he can't. He looks up and lets his eyes drift across the buildings, over broken cement pillars and half balconies, across the buildings' exposed innards: furniture and rugs, doorframes, and crumbled walls and stairs—he's inside a rupture of the very material of creation, and knows he's changed. He doesn't come from Sweden anymore—from its classrooms and suburban streets—he is pure, without history.

He realizes that this is what he's been searching for his whole life.

He might go back to Sweden soon, it could happen. The brothers talk about how actions in the West are needed to wake up Muslims there, the ones who don't get that this is war. He thinks about what it would be like to be in Gothenburg again, how everyone would think he comes from there, when really he no longer comes from anywhere, now that he has been freed.

He wants to roar.

He comes from the moment he shot that first prisoner. He comes from this desolate landscape inhabited by ghosts and flies and dogs, this caliphate where everything is beginning anew. There is no one who can claim to know him anymore, to know who he is. He belongs to no one. He is no one.

A monster.

The rain makes it hard to see. But he doesn't need to see well, just to keep the barrel of the gun pressed to the back of the prisoner's head. The guy's entire body shakes and it still seems like he wants to talk. He mumbles something that sounds like *nonono*, Hamad notes with amusement as he pulls the trigger. He doesn't think it's tears that he keeps wiping away. He feels a pleasing emptiness, a nothing feeling. He looks at the sky for a second. That's when he sees the emblem.

It's one of those extravagant souvenirs that pilgrims buy on their last day in Mecca. The seal is painted in gold against a black background and framed, hanging crooked on a living room wall on the fourth floor, among junk scattered by a rocket attack. *There is no God but God.* Gold Arabic lettering glinting through the rain. *No God.* He feels sick, wobbles, and bends over, hands on his thighs. Everything is spinning, seems to be turning upside down; somehow, he ends up on his knees.

He tries to get up. He's confused, his hands are tied behind his back. Wait. He must've collapsed and the brothers have mixed him up with a prisoner because of his mask.

"Wait," he says. He laughs, he says: "It's me." What a story this'll be later. But wait.

He isn't masked anymore. They should recognize him. But there's a man looming over him in the rain wearing a balaclava. "It's me," he says again, in Arabic, but nobody seems to notice. *Hold on. Fuck. Fuck, come on, it's him.* It's Hamad standing there with a balaclava on, broad shouldered but stooped.

"I'm you," he says, and the man with the gun looks at him. "I'm you!" He's shouting it now, and tries to get up again, but somebody kicks him from behind and he falls, winded, into the mud.

The first shot makes him flinch, and he gets back on his knees. Everything seems reasonable in the way of a nightmare: Hamad over there shoots prisoners number two and three and four, and is now about to shoot himself—he stands behind his kneeling self, the rain running into his mouth tastes like sweat and mud and he looks up at himself, not finding any of what's happening strange in the least. But he's amazed: it's impossible to imagine that you will soon cease to be, in spite of the superficial talk about death that the brothers get into during their free time—heartwarming wishes about martyrdom, so false in the end—he just can't wrap his mind around his own end. He becomes aware of the mass of his organs, the pressure they exert on his pelvis. He understands what it means to be made of clay, of dead matter. He shakes and cries and turns halfway around to look up incredulously at his own masked face. Wants to ask himself to turn back, to become something else once again, but the eyes through the slits in the mask are unrelenting, so foreign, he curls up and says no, no, no. He loves his body because it is all he has. He tries to come up with some detail only he knows, something to shout so Hamad will understand he's about to murder himself.

He got contacts one summer, to fit in, but that's too sick to say, here on a muddy field in Syria a lifetime later.

He looks down. Plumes of water where the rain hits the ground.

I'm you. That's what you are supposed to remember.

We're the same.

A rising roar cut off.

Darkness.

He's in a sack. Who has put me here? Is this the grave? Am I dead now? He thinks he hears somebody sniffling, maybe a woman. He can smell damp earth and feels a terrible pressure on his chest.

He opens his eyes.

Five men with their hands tied behind their backs are kneeling in front of him.

A grenade explodes in a neighborhood nearby, shaking the ground.

"We made the right choice." Isra put a moving box down. A patch of white winter light was reflected in the glossy parquet floor.

We'd been living with friends for a couple of weeks before finding an apartment one stop away from the area in Hasselbo where Amin grew up. I stood there with my moving box as she went to fetch another from the car. Our daughter running, her feet drumming in the empty rooms. I looked out the window at the concrete buildings and empty swings. Stood there for a long time as a ghostly impenetrable sorrow moved through me.

We had stayed.

The girl closed her hands, tight. The baggy clothes, one size too big. Her eyes were dark and sort of wedged beneath her wrinkled forehead. She relaxed her fists, then clenched them.

"This is Isra." We were in the doorway, and I couldn't tell if she even registered our presence. "My wife. You wanted to meet her."

Her fists relaxed, clenched.

An orderly sat in a chair next to her, a man with a high hairline and a watchfulness about him that made me suspect she'd recently had a violent episode.

"I don't speak Swedish," she said in English, low, without looking up, and though I wasn't surprised that her voice sounded different than from our meetings, I felt rejected. Like she was punishing me for some shortcoming, something I should've said while we still had time.

"Do you remember me?"

She shook her head, and started wringing her hands, agitated, like she was trying to tear her own fingers off.

One day in March, as the snow melted and the migratory birds returned, a girl with dark bushy hair sat in one of the swings, wearing only overalls and a T-shirt. I saw her through my office window and called to my daughter, who'd been having a hard time making friends here, telling her to go outside. Soon, she was walking across the playground, head bare, winter jacket open. She climbed onto the swing next to the new girl. They started talking and soon their laughter rolled in through my window.

We stayed because we owed that girl in the asylum a feeling of hope. Because everything was different because of her. We stayed with the gravel fields and misty rain, with the power lines and contrails, with our living and our dead.

My daughter sat on her bed. A glass mobile hung in her window, a souvenir from one of Isra's trips to Algeria many years before. The pieces were shards of window glass and bottles polished by the Mediterranean; they spun slowly round and round, casting dancing colored flares across the walls and over my daughter's arms and face, set deep in concentration.

She was still so close to the beginning that I could watch her for hours, because I sensed the roar against her outer walls.

She was playing with a string—a long cord she'd found somewhere or coaxed from Isra—pulling it out into a star between her fingers, biting down on one end, pulling it into another shape.

She noticed me and looked up.

"Dad, can you help me? It's for two."

I remember having a sharp headache that day, but otherwise it was a day like any other. The day I finally realized who the girl at the clinic had been. What she always wanted to, but never dared, say.

I sat on my bed, pinching the correct part of the string

without my daughter having to show me, and she laughed with delight.

"You know it?" I nodded. It was the same game the girl from Tundra—who had been my shadow, or my daughter's shadow, or maybe just my daughter—had taught me one rainy day many years ago.

"My new friend showed me," she said. The world did not shake. I felt an incredible despair over what she'd experienced in another world, but also hope—the hope in having stayed, a sibling of the hope that had made my mother cross the sea.

Later, my daughter ran outside into the meltwater and sunshine, still without a history, and I watched her and Liat from the window and remembered her heart on the ultrasound. The gray matchstick-flame flickering on the screen. The underwater drum of life. Allah. God's name.

We stayed with the willow tree, its branches that swayed in the wind. We stayed with the ice crystals on the window glass, with the Swedish social insurance agency and the basement mosques, with rows of preschool children in neon-yellow vests crossing the street. We stayed with the birch-tree pollen that glued itself to the window when spring arrived, and with the melancholy that came deep into summertime.

In the swings they get ready, set, and then jump. Liat and my daughter. I play the video from Hondo's in my office. Hamad is shouting:

"You desecrate Islam!" And I hear it so clearly this last time: most of all he's trying to convince himself. The rage is theater, an attempt to create meaning.

I stay to give my daughter an inheritance other than madness.

I hear the screams, the gun salvos.

I watch them as they swing higher and higher.

This country became our sea.

I turn off the video. Find an audio file from one of my meetings with the girl from Tundra. The static of the clinic. Our breathing.

"Does it scare you that you might stop existing?"

"I've always been afraid," she says, and her voice fills me with a longing so acute that I have to steady myself on the desk so as not to fall to pieces. She's gone now. Gone. My daughter, who saved me. This meeting was one of our last. "When I disappear maybe I'll end up in a place where I'm not afraid anymore."

I remember her smiling as she said it, one of her fleeting smiles.

"Do you remember a place like that? A time before the fear?" I ask on the recording, with all the tenderness I never thought I'd let her hear.

"Maybe in the beginning."

Then we fall silent, and I can hear my daughter and Liat's laughter through the window. They're sitting in the swings, gaining speed before they leap. Our threadbare strips of the future. And when the wind picks up and lifts the sand they just laugh, covering their eyes.

The light ahead.